THE SANDERSON WITCH MUSEUM
FOR RELEASE OCTOBER 15, 1988

FINAL ACQUISITION ARRIVES FROM OLD BURIAL HILL
IN TIME FOR WICKED WITCHES OF SALEM EXHIBIT AT
THE SANDERSON WITCH MUSEUM

This legendary book belonging to the Sanderson
coven was just gifted to the Sanderson Witch
Museum, which will open on October 31. This final
acquisition was found in a crumbling stone wall
outside Old Burial Hill and includes potion
recipes and spells used by witches dating back
to the early 1660s, the last known owner being
Winifred Sanderson. It will be featured as a main
attraction in the exhibit, along with the Black
Flame Candle, but will be placed under glass
to dissuade guests from opening its pages and
delving into its dark and ill-fated contents.

For researchers looking inside this book, please
do not attempt any of the practices mentioned
in this text. The Sanderson Witch Museum cannot
be held accountable for misfortunes that trying
these rituals may bring about.

Yours sincerely,

Rachel Watts

R. Watts
Museum Director

Printed in the United States of America
First Hardcover Edition, August 2022

1 3 5 7 9 10 8 6 4 2

FAC-034274-22203

Library of Congress Control Number: 2022931830

ISBN 978-1-368-07669-2

Designed by Gegham Vardanyan

Visit disneybooks.com

DISNEP

HOCUS POCUS

Spell Book

A GUIDE TO SPELLS, POTIONS, AND HEXES FOR THE ASPIRING SALEM WITCH

Property of Winifred Sanderson
31st of October 1660

Stay out of my book, you little brats!

Written by Eric Geron

DISNEP PRESS

LOS ANGELES · NEW YORK

Master's Pact

A MOST MIRACULOUS WELCOME TO THE WORLD OF WITCHCRAFT.

Why, thank thee, Master!

Master doth solemnly promise to aid thee on thy mystic path to power. Within this ancient tome duly bestowed, thou hast been entrusted to practice the crafting of potions and draughts, and the vocalizing of chants, invocations, hexes, curses, spells, and songs set forth within. These pages shall reveal what thou most seekest, with magick to torment when there is havoc to wreak. Be most patient, for it hath often taken decades for even the most skilled witches to grasp the contents of the book.

I shall be thine advocate.

Pledge of Secrecy

Thou hast dedicated thy life to witchcraft, with thy work coveted above all else as with thine ancestors of witches who have come before. Thy sacrifice for solitude and focus will be worth an eternity of glory. To invoke the path of eternal promise, utter now this sacred vow:

Travel in moonlight, cloak, smoke, shadow, and shade.
Thy journey beginneth now that thy course is set.
Thou must cloak thy truth as thou cloak'st thy blade
and duly vow to keep thy true self secret.

I am a rustle of leaves, a shadow with no form,
A mighty fire with no smoke found to stoke a swarm,
A strange birdsong, a memory that disappears,
A shifting shape, a name lost on lips and ears.
A ripple o'er blue rolling wave,
A flash past window-sill,
A titter causing horse to bray,
A dim chanting o'er hill.

As cloud wreaths moon, may this oath be
a coronet thou shalt don with pride.

Tis the highest honor.

Promise from Thy Spell Book

If ever mine eye doth wake to find us apart *Nooo!*
Whether or not I am pried from thine hand or thy stand
My dark pages shall fast unfurl to illuminate
A pillar of brightest golden light, a most divine strand.

The Incantation to Bind Yourself to This Book:

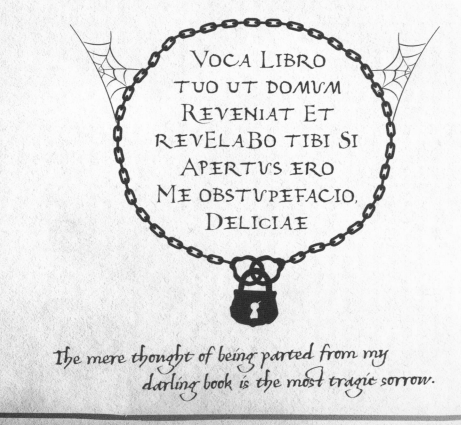

VOCA LIBRO
TUO UT DOMUM
REVENIAT ET
REVELABO TIBI SI
APERTUS ERO
ME OBSTUPEFACIO,
DELICIAE

The mere thought of being parted from my
darling book is the most tragic sorrow.

Message from Thy Spell Book

MY PAGES CAN BE NEITHER BURNT NOR CHARRED

Yes, but the pages can be written upon quite nicely, it seems.

NOR RIPPED NOR DEFILED NOR SLASHED NOR SCARRED *

MY PAGES MAGICK'LY TRANSFORM FOR THEE

TO REFLECT AND TRANSCRIBE THY HISTORY

A book! A book! A book!

I can read! And write! 'Tis a miracle!

It appears the spell book's pages are not impervious to kitten-paw soup stains. . . . Sorry, Winnie.

*I hath learnt my book hast a tongue of fire against those who wouldst do it harm.

Winifred Sanderson

ELDEST SANDERSON SISTER

I prefer "wisest" Sanderson sister, thank you very much.

Winnie the Wicked, born long in the tooth
Simpering, whimpering babe steeped in gloom.
Red hair like flame, thou desirest eternal youth,
Arise now, fire bright'ning with lightning. Grasp broom!
Long-toothed Winnie! Ratty-haired Winnie!
Wild-eyed Winnie! *It really hurteth my feelings!*

There, there, Winnie . . . Wouldst thou allow me to hold thee?

Thou cast cunning paths of smoke-wisp and bone
While shrouded in warm garbs of envy green,
Wakest those long-lost souls whose mouths were sewn
Most wicked leader—clever, crude, and mean.
This cursed coven is indeed my brainchild.
Mmm . . . Brain . . . Child . . .

Thy strength shall flourish when thy deeds art done.
But beware an end in stone, dust, and sun. *Uh-oh.*

FULGUR CAELUM DIVIDIT
ET OMNIA IN VIA DESTRUIT.

Mary Sanderson *Hello!*

MIDDLE SANDERSON SISTER

Mary the Malicious, born round and pink
Grumbling, whining babe crying out for milk
Brown locks like mud of pond, nostrils that flare,
Stuck in shadow of sisters who don't care.

It's fine, I'm fine. My sisters love me.

Forever sniffing for unsavory food
While shrouded in orange and disquietude
Barking for victims before fatal bite
A seeking, hungry muse amazingly bright.

Children are so sweet. I can eat them right up!

Bright?! Ha! Mary is but an addlebrained stockfish.

SPIRATIO
PROFUNDA
NASO OMNIA
POTEST
DETEGERE.

We are famished! Sniff out some children, Sister Mary! Follow thy nose!

'Tis an accurate depiction of me!

I thought I made clear to my doltish sisters to keep their filthy paws off my book!

Though it does impress to discover Sister Sarah has the ability to read and write . . .

Sarah Sanderson

YOUNGEST SANDERSON SISTER

Sarah the Scandalous, born thin and pale
Singing, whispering babe with lucky rat tail
Hair like golden wheat, desiring rav'nous love
Cooing in the passionate sky like a dove

Teasing, tempting, and snaring more than some
While shrouded in silk garbs of sweetest plum
Enchanting dreamers to stumble her way
Boldest temptress—giddy, giggling, and gay.

VOX
CLARA CANIT
SOMNIATORIBUS
IN SOMNIO MALO
PULCHRO.

'Tis I, sisters!

Way of the Red Witch

OW 'TIS TIME TO FULFILL THY ROLE AS WITCH.

How doth one step fully into the life of a Red Witch? Thou must learn the name and color that burneth within thee, the rites and rules of thy coven, the garbs and objects of immense powers. Inside this section thou wilt discover how to establish thy secret abode and how to brew enchanted dishes. These things will help thee uncover the legends of olde, and keep the gleam on the Sanderson Legacy.

Name of Inner Flame

Find thy title to enhance thy true nature
To strike icy fear with nomenclature
To enchant beating hearts to melt or freeze
To bewitch stomachs to lurch and seize

Combine thy first name with a word below
of the same first letter to create thy witchy title,
And keep this one name on the tip of thy tongue.

ABYSMAL	NASTY
BITTER	OBSEQUIOUS
COMPLACENT	PETULANT
DREADFUL	QUIXOTIC
EGREGIOUS	RASH
FECKLESS	SCANDALOUS
GRANDIOSE	TERRIBLE
HEINOUS	UNJUST
IMPRUDENT	VILE
JEALOUS	WICKED
KNAVISH	XENIAL
LOATHSOME	YAWNING
MALICIOUS	ZEALOUS

*Malicious?
But I haven't
a malicious bone
in my body . . .
only the bones
of our prey.*

*"Sarah the
Scandalous"
I love it!!!*

*I am
Winifred
the Wicked!
How
fitting!*

Truest Hue

Choose a color to represent thy core
To lace in boot and hood, cloak and more
To represent the pure hue of thy pith
To magnify thine energy herewith.

Keep this one color close and in abundance:

RED—Deceptive, Evasive,
Illusionary

ORANGE—Greedy,
Hungry, Doltish

YELLOW—Wrathful,
Vengeful, Bitter

GREEN—Prideful, Strong,
Envious

BLUE—Mercurial,
Clandestine, Mysterious

VIOLET—Passionate,
Frivolous, Whimsical

PINK—Brutish,
Tenacious, Solid

*Orange is my color.
I am a greedy dolt.*

*Violet!
Though
it does very
little for my
complexion!*

*I obviously
choose green,
the color of
POWER!*

Wheel of the Red Witch

Before learning spells, connect with a letter from the Wheel of the Red Witch:

B—Befuddlement *What dost this mean, sisters?*
I am terribly confused!

C—Compassion

D—Desperation *I am desperate for*
Winnie's validation.
Did I write that? Oops!

E—Emptiness

F—Fright

G—Glee

H—Humiliation

I—Infuriation *I obviously connect most*
with this letter.

K—Keenness

Use your word from the Wheel in your spells to infuse thy magick with its truculent and turmoiled charge.

Rites of the Red Witch

Thou hast revered the day you became a witch, the day thou chose thy name and color. Thou hast lauded the Master, mourned thy mother's fading cackle.

Thy powers will become heightened with each potion brewed, with each spell cast.

Ev'ry month, host a day of manifestation for thy continued growth, and gratitude for thy blooming fruits of darkness, for the fire and brimstone running richly through thy blood.

Thou must honor and celebrate
the various stages of being
an ascending witch:

WITCH: WE DRESS IN FINEST CLOAKS.

WITCH: WE JOIN HANDS IN A CIRCLE.

WITCH: WE CHANT FOR OUR WISDOM.

Our witchcraft will bear fruit!
Every boy will adore me!!!

Siblinghood of the Red Witch

Lightning in your hot blood,
magick in your boiling brew.
The legacy of the Red Witch
liveth now within you.

Ye have devoted your lives
for your inhuman shield
Your bonds forever fastened,
your fates forever sealed.

Take up your fiery mantles
and blaze the twisted yew
The power of the red flame
shineth valiantly for you.

Becoming a Red Witch
hast been most worthwhile, wouldn't you say, sisters?

Power of the Coven

Being part of a coven nurtureth the power inside

When thou harnessest thy craft with siblings
firm by thy side.

Magick flowing swiftly in blood and bone worketh together

As one witch stoopeth or leaneth to hold up
the other's tether. *I live to serve thee, my dearest sister Winnie.*

Join hands and ranks as one to steel your intended design

As words, spells, and paths weave to form
an unbreakable twine. *I miss my lucky rat tail.*
Where have I left it this time?

Come rigor, vigor, pain, or disdain—lead the winning way

For the coven followeth the call of one without delay.

Thou art part of this lifelong path, this steep-fated game

As thou continuest thy legacy and honorest thy name.

*I wish to leave my doltish sisters in the dust and strike
out on my own! Alas . . . I must do as the book says.*

Raiment of the Red Witch

Thou shalt adorn thy temple

With ring, boot, and striped sock,

With wand, broom, and velvet frock

With corset cloak of river,

With pointed hood and silver

With wand, belt, skirt, and necklace

With embroidered robes fleckless

To reflect thine inner being.

One is never truly dressed
without contempt on one's tongue.

And a warm cloak of lightweight material.

'Tis a hard garb to come by!

And a most flattering bodice to
capture even the most trained eye!

8th of June 1661

I have noticed witch hunters have begun to gather in the town,
sisters! We must be wary. Take note of their appearance below.

Raiment of Witch Hunters :
- Black robes
- Axes to chop wood
* Do not let them near!

Amulets of Arcane

Amass these engraved charms with marks most mystical, with crystals and gemstones lodged, to adorn thy flesh, to forbid thy foes, to buttress thy magick.

NECKLACE OF MIGHT—With drops of Obscene Obsidian, this necklace when rested across sternum bringeth surplus of confidence.

BUCKLE OF MALICE—Polished tablets of Endless Emerald set within twining fiery snakes clasp together to close, and direct animosity when worn upon waist.

RING OF AMPLIFICATION—Silver band holding Querulous Quartz channels and amplifies deep inner magick.

CUFF OF ACCURACY—Gold studded with Ashen Amethyst, this cuff ensures spells cast have desired effect.

PENDANT OF SIGHT—Embedded with Grisly Garnet, born from the mouth of the Gift Horse, this silver pendant gives ability to see what is unseen.

I wear each with pride. My beau, Billy, says they suit me well, and I quite agree.

& Talismans of Vice

RUIN OF MIM—Tablet of carved stone, this talisman cloaketh thee with the appearance of an owl.

NAUTILUS OF DISCORD—Shell purloineth the voice of thy victim to store within its spiral husk.

GOLDEN SCARAB BEETLE—Golden beetle halves, when joined, open caverns of forbidden entry.

GHASTLY TALISMAN—Pendant taketh a pinch of blood to transform shadows into wraiths.

LAMP OF MAGICK—Of gold and oil, this lamp sheddeth light to illuminate thy wish.

I would store away Sister Sarah's voice if we did not require it to lure children.

My singing voice is unmatched! Just ask Billy. He can listen to me sing for hours!

Billy, Billy, a gentle lad. Billy, Billy, a dapper cad. Billy, Billy, wiggle thy toes. Billy, Billy, nobody knows!

Tail of Rat
GOOD LUCK CHARM

From vermin squalid and slick
Carrying flea, tick, and sick,
A tail most wormlike to chew
For halcyon times anew.

My lucky rat tail! I found it! It was right where I left it! In the loft above the door!

Works like a charm!
And still has its tangy flavor! Mmmm!

Flayed Tongue of Adder

ABUNDANCE OF FORTUNE

Snake of charm with coils black
From its fangs a forked tongue slack
To plant in soil dry as bone
For bounty sown and prize new-grown.

I did as Winnie instructed
and planted the tongue for good fortune,
but all it seemed to do was sprout
the most unsightly mushrooms . . .
which went well with my carcass pot pie.

Jagged Black Coal

ENDLESS MISFORTUNE

A stone webbéd in dark fate
Lustrous with loss and dire strait
A charm to mar, char, and scar
For light rays thou wishest most to bar.

Marvelous! I shall use this coal on those miserable townsfolk.

*That will teach them to mind their business
and stop nosing around our woods.*

Yeah! Nosing around is MY job!

Fang of Dire Mole

WITHERING CROPS

From thine hole of dusk and din
Wrinkle-faced with curséd grin
From its maw a fang cobalt
To blight the earth as if with salt.

Oooh, this would explain why the herb garden withered.
I must have dropped it when Sister Sarah bumped
me while dancing.

Thou art always getting in the way
of my frolicking, Sister Mary.

Relics of Repute

The relics of Red Witches of Yore connect thee to thy past. May the relics inspire thy spellcasting and magick, thine intentions and purpose, thy fated calling in the Red Legacy.

VEIL OF MATHILDA PICARDY
Torn from Mathilda's burial place,
The linen cloth beareth her face.

Such a clever little witch . . .
but not clever enough,
unfortunately for her.

EYE OF AMICE HARVEY
Eye for an eye duly plucked,
Pressed into thy book's construct.

Traitorous troll!
He had it coming!

CAULDRON-SPOON SPLINTER OF FRANCES HARVEY

Splinter with a wealth of magick,
Tracéd from a life most tragic.

CHAINS OF CECILY SANDERISSON

Surviving flame and harsh exile,
Links untarnished from the trial.

Perhaps witches cannot burn!

Oh. we mustn't find out. Sister.

These tales fill me with such sweet sorrow.

Cheer up, Winnie. Thou wouldst have made them most proud.

Scepters of Standing

DARK FAIRY SCEPTER
Used to curse with thorns of fear,
Twisted staff and emerald sphere.

SEA WITCH TRIDENT
Used to rule the ocean cold,
Three-pronged rod of stormy gold.

Perfect for prodding Mary's backside!

SORCERER SNAKE STAFF
Used to trick and hypnotize,
Head of cobra, ruby eyes.

Broom
of the
Red Witch

Filch sturdy branch of oak or of pine
To whittle and carve, burnish and shine;
Next, bind twigs to the end with string
Rudder for sailing, and now thou wilt cling.
On stick lightweight, catch wind and fly,
And cut through downy cloud high in the sky.

I find a new broom flies clean.

I use mine to sweep things
under the rug! That is, when
Winnie isn't sweeping me aside.

Broom, ho!
I hope someone sweeps me off my feet!

Familiars of the Red Witch

To assist thee with thy magickal practices, the Master doth provide a familiar to each Red Witch. These loyal spirits take many forms: The red-eyed rat for spying on thy behalf. The sticky-footed toad for finding thy lost items. The fanged owl to fetch thy parcels. The hellion hare to guide thy daily actions. The black hound to guard thy cottage and protect thy life-force. Choose which familiar doth best suit thy needs.

Once seasoned and sage, thou wilt be able to transform into an animal familiar thyself, be it white mouse, brown marten, black cat, yellow bird, hen, or hawk.

BIRDS—Migration, perches and pines

BEETLES—Spying, secretive and out of sight

I have a terrible allergy to familiar dander. I break out in these horrible hives on my neck that I can't seem to stop scratching, and it lasts for a good week at least.

CATS—Light feet, stealth and silence

DOGS—Safety, glaring and growling *Grrrrr!*

EELS—Aquatic ease, winding and weaving

OWLS—Power in patience, swooping and snatching

MOTHS—Aflutter, swift and small

RATS—Condensed, wriggling and scampering

I want a puppy!
    Please. Winnie?
Let me play with one!

Ugh. Feral, flea-bitten miscreants have no place here!

Besides, we already have Mary and her incessant barking.

Abode of the Red Witch

NOW WITH POWERFUL RITES
ESTABLISHED, 'TIS TIME TO SET
UP THY WITCH'S ABODE.

Thou needest an abode to gather together as a coven. Traverse to glen or vale with the thump of paw and call of crow, past the rushing of brackish water over large stones, through the shade of ferns fast unfurling. Ensure none will be able to find thee as thy coven meets beneath full moon. Clearings of trees reveal more than stars. Keep this place sacred and secret.

Secret!
Secret!
I have a secret!

Map of Salem

Witching Woods

Trees, shrubs, bushes, and flowers of the woods provide vital ingredients for magickal brews incomplete. Pick, pluck, and pilfer seeds, fruits, stems, and stalks for thy witchy biddings. Study the movements and forms of beasts of feather and fur until they become as one with thy blood. The land thou chose to be thy witching woods will have all thou needest. Thou shalt be the only one able to find thy way within. Reclused in thy dark and giving Witching Woods, thou art home.

Ah, my place of peace and quiet to concentrate—
when my blundering sisters are not fending.

Clandestine Cottage

Once deep in the woods,
as not to be found,

By a stream that winds
and weaves underground,

But also close by
to village and town,

And close enough
to lure a child!

To spy and watch and
stalk around,

We love having
children over for
dinner....

Find a spot in the woods
to call thine own,

To build a cottage quaint
with stick and stone.

Inside, a vaulted room
to cast and cook.

Rafters, shelves, and
latticed windows to look.

And a loft upstairs
for bedding!

Mirthful Hearth

Like how the bird gathereth twigs for its nest,

Collect woody broom, cupboard, crate, and chest,

A fire to stoke, black cauldron to fill,

Spoons for stirring, cups heaped high with swill,

A stand for thy book, candles on thy sill,

Iron cages for birds from which to trill,

A staff or stick, a chair from which to eat,

Ropes to restrain enemies, a vial, a sheet.

Extra-strength!

8th of November 1663

Since settling in Salem, we have started luring
children our way so we might practice our spells.

Sniff out more of the brats, Sister!

Yes, Winnie. Mmm . . . Young blood . . .
My mouth is watering already.

I shall work my *magick*,
and prance to town to collect them!

The Altar

Erect a table of maple, oak, or pine

To powder root, crush nut and seed, and clip vine

To lay down thy cloth and magick possessions

To dress with shriveled flowers of thy sessions

To adorn with artifacts of the caster

For the dark work of the eternal Master.

I have left more than a few at the altar, sisters!

Altar Tools

Clear the altar of all, till bare

Now place water cup, strand of hair

Next fix stick of sturdy black oak

Then lay rotten egg without yolk.

I shall let my *nosy* sister bother with the table preparations.

Of course, Winnie. Sorry, Winnie. Right away!

And I shall dance about the table!

Black Cauldron Magick

There is nothing like wafting the woodsy smell of a fresh batch of cauldron brew!

Witches require a portly vessel in which to churn their bewitching brews, their simmering stews, and their percolating potions. Thy cauldron acteth as a basin to house thy wild'st endeavors.

Make sure thy cauldron be black, and grand, suspended on chain and with flames 'neath for the melting of mixtures and the cooking of enchanted dishes. Keep the largest main cauldron at room center and others along the wall.

Our main cauldron is hard to clean after. Not that I would know. I leave the dirty work to Mary, that frowzy fopdoodle. Sisters, let us brew a new plot!

I have found good old water and vinegar make for an effective cleaner.

Vial Things

Prepare thine home for the infusing and seeping of potions. Gather stocks of ingredients, stores of jars and bottles to brim, thine own private rations. Brews . . . Elixirs . . . Spells . . .

Gather to thyself the plants, herbs, insects, and animals of thy Witching Woods. Create oils, essences, and tinctures fundamental for any witch to possess.

Vials of things for vile things of thy wile . . .

Vial Things

 ARROWROOT
ANTENNAE OF ANT
ANCHOVY

My beau, Billy, just gifted me with a new stock. What a faithful gentleman. And most generous...

 **BLEEDING HEART**
BLOWFLY
BUCKTHORN OIL

 CASTOR OIL
CRABAPPLE
CROCODILE JAW

Crabapple-and-maggot pie! My favorite (besides humble pie)!

 DITTANY
DANDELION OIL
DUNG BEETLE

I should check our rations. You never know when Winnie will want to brew something up!

Vial Things

 ESSENCE OF SHREW
EVERLASTING OIL
EYE OF NEWT

 FORGET-ME-NOT
FLAXSEED
FANG OF FLEA

The boys never forget me when I am through with them ... because they are dead!

 GORSE
GOLDENSEAL OIL
GIZZARD OF TURKEY

I still have scars from when this was my nickname. **It hurts even now!**

There, there, Winnie ...

 HAWTHORN
HOUND'S-TONGUE
HONEYSUCKLE

A boy once told me my singing was like honeysuckle on the ear!

I miss him. He wore his heart on his sleeve!

And it was delicious!

Vial Things

IRIS *I knew an Iris once.*
IVY OIL *A most delectable little child.*
IRONWEED

JICAMA
JELLYFISH TENTACLE
JEWELWEED

KNOTWEED
KATYDID
KALE *This provides most excellent roughage,*
and goes well in a blend of strawberries,
bananas, and ice.

LARVA OF MOTH
LOCUST
LARD *Lard!*

Vial Things

 MOLASSES
MILLIPEDE
MORNING GLORY*

Ooh. I love how they ~squeak~ when I sink my teeth in them!

 NETTLE
NUTMEG OIL
NEWT SALIVA

Mary needs to tend to my stores. I appear to be running rather low on my inventory.

Yes, Winnie! Right away! I am inept!

 OIL OF BOIL
OCHRE
ONION

 POPPY SEED
PUS OF PICKLED EGG
PUMPKINSEED OIL
Puppy Love!

*Mary's
Pickled Egg Recipe:*

1. *Peel rotten egg.*
2. *Plop egg in pus.*

Thou hast forgotten the pickle!

*Makes me sick.

Vial Things

 QUEEN BEE *A creature after my own wicked heart.*
QUAKING GRASS
QUINCE

 ROOT OF RHUBARB
ROSEMARY *I hate her!*
RICE WEEVIL *She stole the affections of the milliner's son from me!*

 SLUG *Poor little misunderstood being.*
SACRED HEART
SNAPDRAGON

 TOOTH OF TARANTULA
TARRAGON
TINCTURE OF TURMERIC

Vial Things

 UNDERWING OF VULTURE
UNICORN ROOT
ULNA

 VIOLET *I hate her too!*
VALERIAN
VERVAIN

 WOLFSBANE
WITCH HAZEL
WART OF HOG

The bane of wolves, perhaps, but a particular favorite of mine . . .

Winnie is always saying we are the bane of her existence.

 XANTHISMA
XIMENIA CAFFRA
XYLODROMUS

These all sound so appetizing, Winnie!

Vial Things

 YARROW
YUCCA
YELLOWJACKET   *Yellow jacket?*
                        But we do not possess any
                                 jackets that are yellow!

 ZEST OF SALAMANDER
ZEDOARY
ZUCCHINI

*Sister Sarah merely chants the name of
each ingredient and gets in the way of our
brewing.*

Note to Self: **Never use salt!**

Thou art so very wise, Winnie!

What about pepper? I love pepper!

Of Leg & Ligament

Passed a body down into dirt
Fell a soul into the shadow
From this body pieces taken
Hence thy new ingredients added.

Clipped a fat thumb and dried-up tongue
Stripped a sinew and fingernail
And a wart and bursting boil,
And a lobe and lustrous eyeball.
Then ev'ry leg and ligament
Elbow and knee and lock of hair
Placed in cauldron swirling with mist
Doth fulfill potions and brews.

I keep a handbasket filled
to the brim of
such delightful digits.

Some are more ripe
than others. . . .
Winnie, we just
got some fresh ones!

Dead Man's Toe

When churning a broth
of contents impure
Drop a dead man's toe
From thy hidden store.

Dead man's toe!
Dead man's toe!
Dead man's toe!

Enchanted Dishes of Red Witches

ON THE ENCHANTED DISHES OF WITCHES, FOR THE GURGLING AND GRUMBLING GUT,

The concoctions and confections of the Red Witch. Their dishes ensnare and enrapture, their ingredients potent. Here within are some of the dishes with lingering tastes and lasting effects.

Now with fine ingredients gathered, 'tis time to prepare these dishes bewitched.

A Proper Witch Kitchen

Crow's Wing Porridge

A DISH TO SUP WHEN SUN IS UP,
WITH GRIT LIKE SILT IN STAGNANT STREAM.

Mmm, a family favorite!
It smells like swamp 'neath a hot sun!

Wing of crow.
Pour forth a bounty of oats;
Stop, a rush of water;
Stop, a spurt of black venom;
Dash of amaranth, stir thrice.
One thing left and 'tis complete,
add the scales of raven's feet.

Oh! Crow! I eat crow!

My specialty is candy crow to lure
the children to our cottage!

Witch's Noodle Soup

WHEN THY BODY IS STRICKEN SICK WITH CRICK,
MAKE THIS CRUELEST SOUP TO SOOTHE THYSELF.

Carrots.

Pour forth broth of black river;

Stop, a smidgen of pigeon,

Dash of salt and pepper,

Pinch of onion, clove, celery,

Oil of boil, and thyme; stir once.

One thing left and 'tis prepared,

add a dollop of child scared.

Snot-nosed brats!

27th of March 1664

'Tis perfect for a cold and rainy day such as this.

Perfect like thee, Sister!
And tastier than kitten-paw stew!

Rat-Paw Pottage

A STEW OF SPLENDOR MOST TENDER
WHEN HUNGER DOTH PLAGUE THY STOMACH.

Rats.

Pour forth water from stream;

Stop, a potato peeled and snout grated;

Stop, a chunk of meat and mat of fur;

Stop, the two long teeth, the claws;

Pinch of pus from oozing boil,

Drop of ulcer, stir fivefold.

When mist gloweth black, do not speak
and listen for sound of squeak.

This dish requires great stamina and strength
to churn the ladle, but the wonderful nutty aroma
makes the efforts not in vain!
And the flaky crust that forms on top
is simply scrumptious!

Centipede *
Chowder

WHEN NIGHTS ARE OLD AND COLD,
FILL THY TEMPLE WITH MOST WRIGGLING WARMTH.

Centipedes, whole.

Pour forth potatoes mouldy;

Stop, a rush of spoiled milk;

Stop, a clove of garlic and onion;

Pinch of thyme and bay leaf,

Dash of flour, salt and
pepper, stir eightfold.

Ladle out and eat while hot
with consistency of snot.

*This one makes me
squirm with delight!*

* *Exchange centipedes with kittens for kitten-paw stew!*

Maggot-Apple Pie*

A TREAT TO EAT WHEN WANTING SWEET,
WITH MAGGOTS WRITHING IN JELLY VISCOUS.

Such a pie thou
dost prepare, used
to poison maiden fair:

Rotten apples.

Pour forth bale of oats;

Stop, a shake of flour,

Dash of salt and nutmeg,

Pinch of cinnamon,
stir thrice.

Serve o'er most malod'rous crust,
with dollop of crisped dust. Mmm . . . Crisped dust . . . It goes well on toast!

* Works just as well with scorpions,
like what Mother would make.
Ahh. Mother. Mother. Mother.

Billy is the apple of my eye!
I hope he dost not mind that I am rotten to the core!

Witch's Trifle

A FOOD TO MAKE THY VICTIM QUAKE, STARTING WITH
DELIGHTFUL BITE AND NIPPING TO DOOMÈD CLOSE.

For desserts most just. Above the flames,
the bubbling cauldron.

Lard.

Add sprinkle of water and milk;

Stop, powdered root of rhubarb;

Stop, thirteen cups of sugar;

Stop, lady's fingers,

Pinch of vanilla, stir fifteenfold.

When 'tis thick and towers tall,
season with tiny things that crawl.

Pudding!

*Sister Mary
always seems to
bite off more than
she can chew.*

*Well, Sister Sarah never helps with the preparations.
She is always off to town.*

*To lure the children! 'Tis a chore of utmost importance
appointed by thee, Sister Winnie. I am great with children!*

Legends of Red Witches

ON THE LEGENDS OF RED WITCHES OF YORE, FOR THY REMEMBERING AND THY RELISHING,

The great Witches of Yore shan't be forgotten. Their legends teach, their legacies echo, their tragedies were not in vain. Here within are some of their stories subsequently laid out.

Witches that run amok face bitter ends, but only when caught. Read these passages and heed their tribulations.

Amok! Amok! Amok!

Legend of Gunnilda Arden

GUNNILDA THE GRANDIOSE, soothsayer in splendid garb, summoned by the prophet, appeared in the forest, And fished a ghoul from the ether, And spoke the ill-fated scene, And the prophet forsook her, And the battle was lost, And so the prophet slashed a blade of blame, But Gunnilda avoided the sword, Lodged in stone, And took flight, And soared 'neath golden moon, And she spake the words which follow: "The victory is mine," And turned the prophet into a worm.

Legend of Eve Harvey

EVE THE EGREGIOUS, fortune-teller to royalty, wife to Amice, mother to two, sold stocks of potions in secret, And her husband passed, And so too the duchess, And Eve was charged for the poisons found, And so she was tortured, But did not confess, And melted the king's image in wax, And the king in turn vanished from his throne without a trace, And when they found the melted wax, they sent for her, Finding her cell empty, And at the castle, the royal babe plucked from his crib.

Legend of Emma Sanderisone

EMMA THE ENVIABLE, beautiful and kind, owner of rodent, was accused of possessing a wicked familiar, For when the plague hit, She was blamed and bound in a mask of shame, So she invoked the wisdom of the Graeae, And gazed into the eye of Medusa, And saw her execution was near, So she called upon the infect'd rats, Who gnawed her bridle, And she lay torpid 'neath brackish lake, Until the plague had passed.

Hast thou heard the rumor that Master is dating Medusa?

Legend of Druscilla Sanderson

DRUSCILLA THE DREADFUL, healer to the Scottish king, sparking the lightning from fingertips, Blamed for scorching tree and raking home, Sought out Morgan le Fay and conspired to foil quests of rotten knights, But they two were caught and banished from the court, And so Druscilla left Avalon to call the Master for counsel, And wove chancy storms to disrupt royal voyage, And saw fate in her enchanted silver mirror, And allowed her spirit to bolt up to moon red as blood.

18th of October 1665
What would Mother say
if she saw us now?
"I am disappointed in you two."
She would say thou art perfect, Winnie.

Legend of Hallowed Ground

Curse that hallowed ground!

Be wary of Hallowed Ground, for
a witch cannot step foot onto grave sites,
the echoing crypts, the burial hills,
the terra-miasma of the dead. . . .

Legend of Ring of Salt

Heed this: a ring of salt
can keep thy power from thy victim.

Mother used to say we were salt of the earth.

Or was it the salt of **her** earth…?

Should we take this with a grain of salt, sisters?

The Natural World of the Red Witch

ON THE NATURAL WORLD OF WITCHES, FOR THY EXPLORING AND THY REAPING,

The natural world giveth innumerable resources and charms. The night sky feedeth thy magick, with the waxing and waning moon, with the constellations of stars, with the distant planets, with the four elementals. The natural world bristleth for thee with many powers known and unknown.

Take what thou needest from realm o'ergrown with riches of dirt and sky, fruit and coarse drupe.

The best fruit is forbidden!

This word truly makes me shudder! I have begun to notice wrinkles marring my beautiful face as I age. The horror!

A Witch in Her Element

Precious Stones

Lustrous or without polish
Singular* or in cluster
These gems possess qualities
Mirac'lous and mysterious.

*Singular is always more powerful, I feel.
Thou canst not spell witchcraft without "I."

I wish for boys to find me lustrous once more!

GRISLY GARNET—Treachery

ASHEN AMETHYST—Calamity

DARK DIAMOND—Apathy

ENDLESS EMERALD—Certitude

I have always been drawn to this ravishing rock.

ARID AQUAMARINE—Detriment

It matches thine eyes perfectly, Sister Winnie.

REPULSIVE RUBY—Vengeance

POX-RIDDEN PEARL—Corruption

PERILOUS PERIDOT—Wreckage
This stone seems to work well on homes of others.

CRUDE CITRINE—Ruination

SINISTER SAPPHIRE—Abandonment

TEMPESTUOUS TOURMALINE—Forfeiture

TRUCULENT TURQUOISE—Eradication

& Crystals of Power

Hold over cauldron smoking
To exhale thine intention.
Place in a bowl of pond slime
And let soak for a fortnight.

9th of October 1666

Let mine intention be crystal clear, sisters: I wish to stay young and be more beautiful.

Thou already art a vision! But there is always room for improvement, of course.

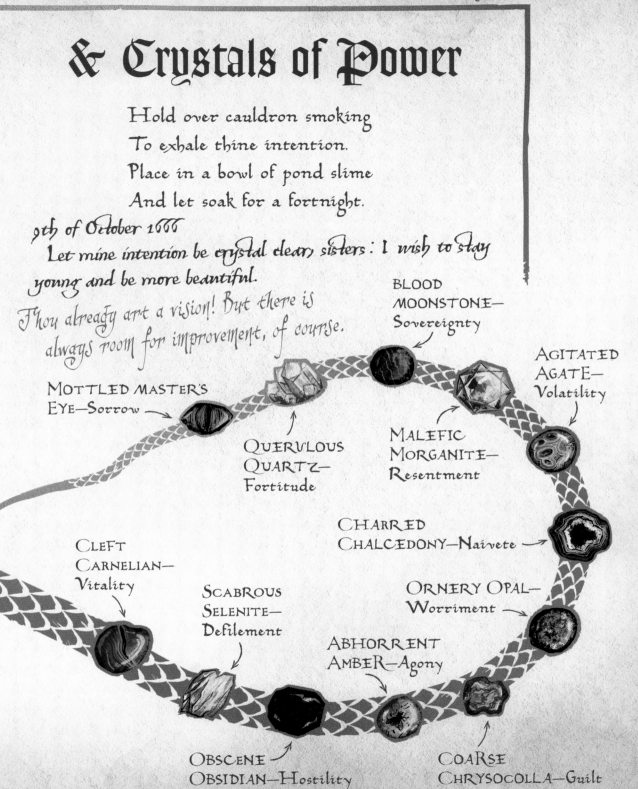

BLOOD
MOONSTONE—
Sovereignty

AGITATED
AGATE—
Volatility

MOTTLED MASTER'S
EYE—Sorrow

QUERULOUS
QUARTZ—
Fortitude

MALEFIC
MORGANITE—
Resentment

CHARRED
CHALCEDONY—Naïvete

CLEFT
CARNELIAN—
Vitality

SCABROUS
SELENITE—
Defilement

ORNERY OPAL—
Worriment

ABHORRENT
AMBER—Agony

OBSCENE
OBSIDIAN—Hostility

COARSE
CHRYSOCOLLA—Guilt

Enlivening of Gemstones

Awaken the power of gemstones by placing in midnight stream 'neath moon and star, for the night imbueth with energy almighty. By wrapping tightly in swathes of thy witchy color and powering with breath and song, only then will thy stones become enlivened with thy charge.

Store for thine eventual spell or hex. Wear as one donneth jewel for maximized power and protection pure. Place 'neath bed or pillow, under floor or overhead, to take effect on thy prey.

I used mine for a love spell on Winnie's beau Billy Butcherson. He is so tall and handsome.

Winnie, pray do not read this!

Blood Moonstone

Passed down most coveted stone

Hidden away, site unknown

Given from mother to child

With heart most tame and mild

If ever stone and witch split

Only one can summon it.

BE WARNED:

IF THE BLOOD MOONSTONE IS BROKEN

OR UNDONE, SO TOO IS EV'RY SPELL

CAST BY SANDERSON.

Mother hath refused to tell me the spell to locate the rotten stone! Blast!

Stones of Future-Seeing

To see future by candlelight, place hands,
eyes, and breath on crystal,
with utterance of the mystic words:

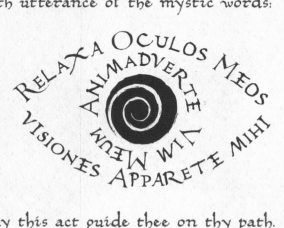

May this act guide thee on thy path.

I saw . . . "driver's permits"
and . . . "Screamin' Jay Hawkins"?
'Tis nonsense!

I think it worked, Sister.
I saw something delicious called
"margarine," and . . . "barbecues"!

It worked for me too, Winnie!
I saw our future!
And thou wert beautiful as if carved from stone!

Prerequisites of Channeling

Breathe into crystal until thy color doth appear inside it. Gaze and see the Master within, and hear his voice. Thereupon access the rousing knowledge of thy long-lost ancestors.

What I would give for just one dance with Master!

Certain wretched ancestors are better left dead, thank you.

Practice the sending of energy. Hold and point crystal. Next repeat thy raucous thoughts in thy mind and silently guide them to thy target until thence stricken. Dread . . . Envy . . . Sorrow . . .

Rehearse the receiving of energy. Lift crystal in open palms, close thine eyes, and breathe deep. Allow the intention of thy sibling to land within thy crystal. Once the gem warmeth in thy palm, open thine eyes. Only then will the crystal contain their essence used to amplify thy spells and hexes.

May these practices be the start of focused intention later put forth to flourish thy magick using crystals.

& Healing Puissance

To revivify and renew, arrange thy stones and crystals into formations to strengthen thy salve and to poultice thine inflictions.

STAR OF STRENGTH—
For mending might

I wish I could restore my youth but by a few years. I feel age creeping up on me!

EYE OF VISION—
For restoring sight

MOON OF MENDING—
For repairing blight

MOTH OF ILLUMINATION—
For replenishing light

FANG OF EDGE—
For sharpening bite

Down, doggy! My bark is worse than my bite!

It giveth Sister Winnie the most terrible headaches.

The Night Sky

ASTRONOMIA

Cosmos existeth for shining with both the fixed and wand'ring stars that pierce the heav'nly vault. Allow for the night sky to act as thy trove of celestial objects from which to spin thy witchy yarns. Join the stars of age-old constellations, and siphon starlight for thy spells and talismans, thy potions and amulets, thy mystic traps to cage life's frothing and flapping rat.

The moon is a most bright object!

Unlike thee, Sister! ... Doth the sun rise in the west?

My sisters are great buffoons!

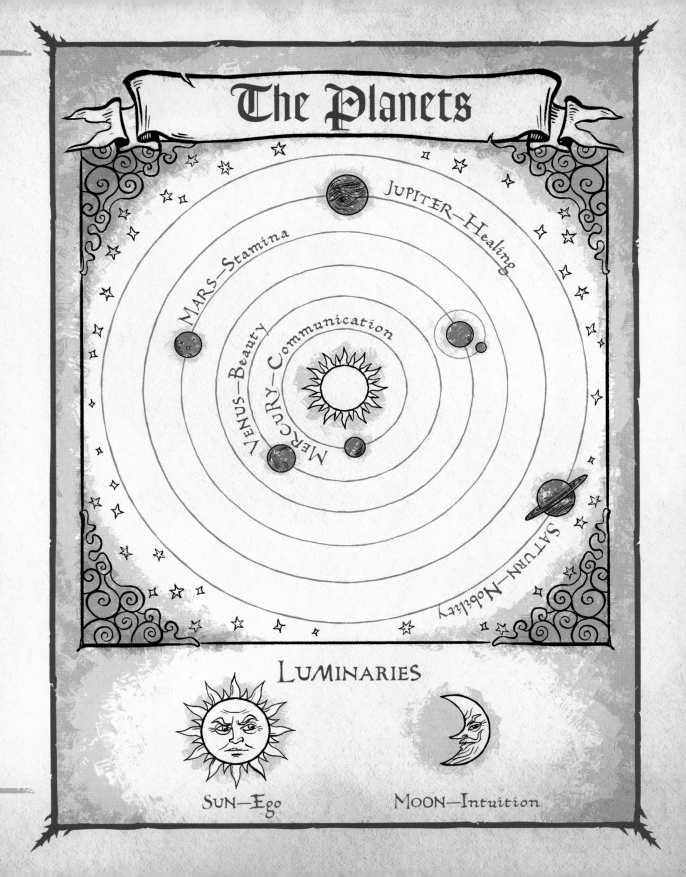

The Planets

JUPITER—Healing

MARS—Stamina

VENUS—Beauty

MERCURY—Communication

SATURN—Nobility

LUMINARIES

SUN—Ego

MOON—Intuition

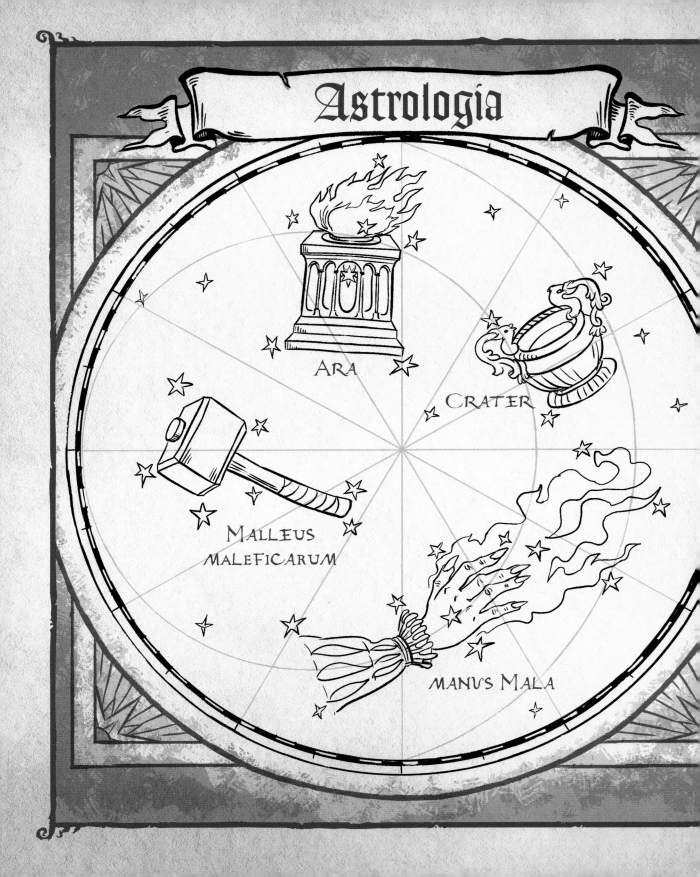

STELLA DIABOLI

SAPIENS *I love flying among the stars!*

REMUS
CHARONIS

The Moon Phases

Mother of witches, pregnant with power,
pitch dark as the night, newly shorn hour;
brighter and growing, harness thy desire;
full and round beacon of mayhem and fire;
sweet light into dark, the glowing sour,
Moon of greatness, gifting thee with power.

3rd of January 1669: We miss thee so, Mummy!   Mother

Mother . . .

Not a cruel night goeth by when I do not
look to the moon and see her looking down on us.

The Elements

The elements are used to guide and channel thy magick.
Harness their abilities by working them into thy senses.

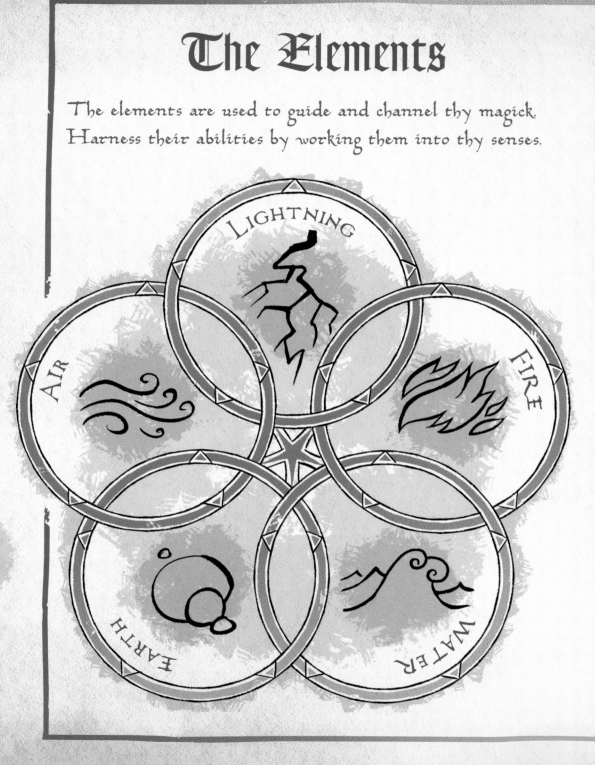

Energy of Earth

Trembled the earth with mighty mountain
Trembled thine hand with the blood-stained dirt
Rising from dust to fall back to dust   *Ugh. Dust!*
By this practice an earthly bond formed.

Start with the quick sinking, sucking mud
Next, tendril unfurling at thy touch   *It worketh, sisters!*
Skipping pebbles o'er rushing brook
Turn stone and rock with single look
Move massive boulder from thy path
By this element a golem forge *Drat!* *All I seem to forge*
Thereupon a trench born from mountain *is a pile of*
Thereupon a clawing tree born from bud. *blasted rocks!*

Virtue of Air

Our sister Sarah is full of hot air.

Blast of air under broomstick, the ride
Veiled key to levitation and flight
Conjuring dark vapor to mask and hide
By this practice an airy bond formed.

Thou art masterful on thy broom, Winnie!

Begin with breath puffing, the chill cloud
Next, the halt to wisp and icy draft
Next, howling gust blustering from thee
Summoning windstorm and the whirlwind
The twisting air that taketh from all
The calamitous gale that toppleth.

The only air Mary can conjure up is an air most natural and smelling of pickled egg!

Strength of Water

Surged the water with mellifluous hiss
Pulling debris down in thine undertow
Leaping geyser burst from deep to fall
By this practice a wat'ry bond formed.

Begin with light
lapping, tracing

Then, honeysuckle
dew, drop of rain

Draining from leaf,
drawing from its vein

Ripple puddles with
thy swell of power

Damming, then ebbing
and flowing forth

Whirling pool, witch-
tossed sea of chaos

Thy power swelling,
thy crest curling

The icy flood, thy
dark waters deep.

Force of Fire

Conjuring the sun in thy cool palm
Melting ice and steel at thy caress
Feeding kindling, strangling inferno
By this practice a fiery bond formed.

Whose son?
The metalworker's son?
I must try this conjuring!

Start with spark
without a hewn flint

Next, cool flame licketh
at thy fingertips

Stoke the glow to heat
thy hearth

Singeing a pyre with
the spark of flame

By this element a
scorching smoke

Thereupon a blaze
born from embers

Thereupon a wildfire
born from ashes.

FIRE! I have
a strong distaste for it.

Legacy of Lightning

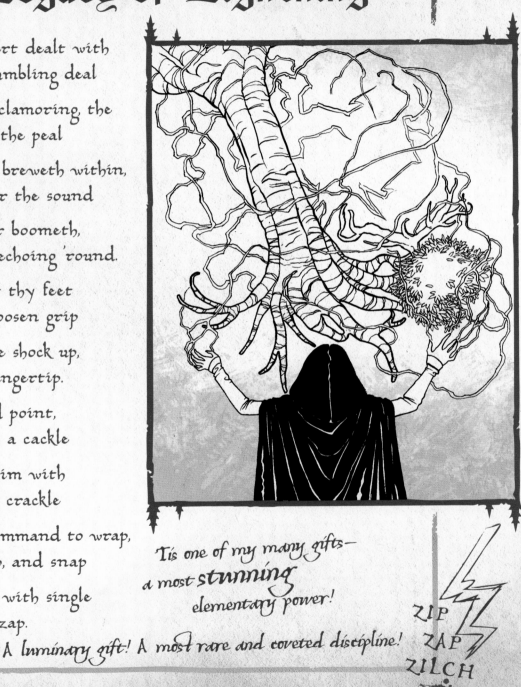

Thou wert dealt with
a rare rumbling deal

Distant clamoring, the
clapping, the peal

A storm breweth within,
strain for the sound

Thunder boometh,
roaring, echoing 'round.

Connect thy feet
solidly, loosen grip

Draw the shock up,
foot to fingertip.

Aim and point,
a branch, a cackle

Lift victim with
brilliant crackle

Then, command to wrap,
trap, slap, and snap

Destroy with single
sizzling zap.

*'Tis one of my many gifts—
a most **stunning** elementary power!*

A luminary gift! A most rare and coveted discipline!

ZIP
ZAP
ZILCH

The Unnatural World of the Red Witch

ON THE UNNATURAL WORLD OF WITCHES, FOR THY SURVIVING AND THY THRIVING,

Past the veil of the living existeth a realm ringed in emerald flame, scorched in scourge and ablaze with anguish, alive with cacophony of caterwauling and cajoling, of crying and cursing. As a Red Witch, thou hast alighted upon its basalt flags, hast traversed its bridges of burning and flaying rope. This tarry under-world teemeth with scabrous beasts and greats of the Beyond, and wayward souls do roam its stony Red Sea Shore, some who never return to the cooled firmament on high, and those who do, passed through the green flame not quite unscathed.

I found it quite lovely to go to the Beyond and back.
Minus the blood-sucking fireflies. Little pests.

The Beyond

The Beyond is a place where witches roam, alight with the green flame. Shadows pool, and eyes watch in darkness, a sense of solitude dashed by the ruckus of rustling and scraping. For the Beyond brimmeth with beasts most terrifying, creatures that lie in wait, ready to pounce and devour.

Witches stay, forever doomed and perpetually determined to escape the furies of its nine realms. Some witches with fortune blessed are able to leave, to carry out the Master's craft far above.

Master is in the details!

Returning from the Beyond

Once thou hast walked through lanes of lonely shadows
Through dreary towns, past lava in hissing rivulets
Like walking in the woods without a sliver of moon,
Darkness punctuated by geysers of stinking green fire
Weird monsters, hissing and clad in flame, hunched
In doorways and trees, stirring at the sound of thy
breath . . .

Thou wilt have ventured to the tormented realm; and may
Return yet. Go forth back to the natural world, with land of
Darkness, with rivers of demise, with shores of
Destruction, emboldening thy steadfast step
And return up above in the land of light,
In thy cottage, and find thy cauldron full of new
potentials. . . .

*Winnie, I'm
scared.*

Gods of the Beyond

The gods possess enviable powers, magicks that no one witch can comprehend. . . .

Each god hath their own unique trait. . . . Which wilt thou call upon for thine aid?

DIONYSUS
GOD OF GRAPE CULTIVATION

NEMESIS
GODDESS OF SHADOW VENGEANCE

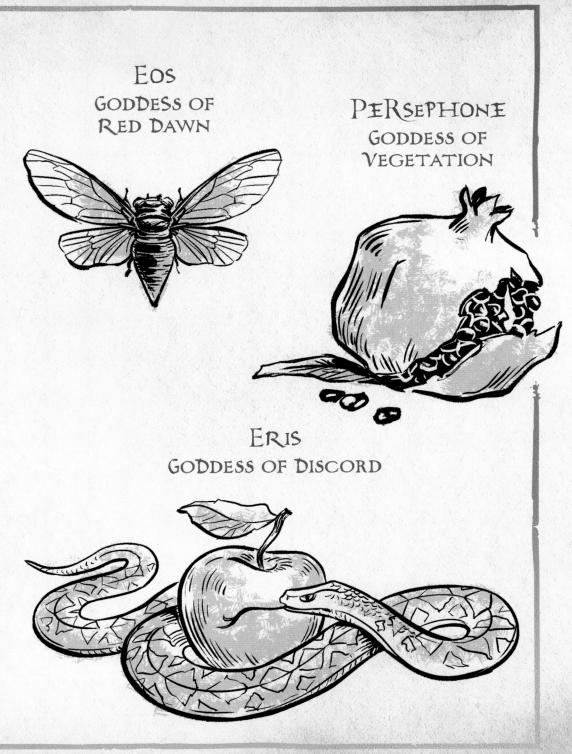

EOS
GODDESS OF
RED DAWN

PERSEPHONE
GODDESS OF
VEGETATION

ERIS
GODDESS OF DISCORD

Gods of the Beyond

HEBE
GODDESS OF YOUTH

I wish very much to be acquainted with this one.

HELIOS
GOD OF SUN

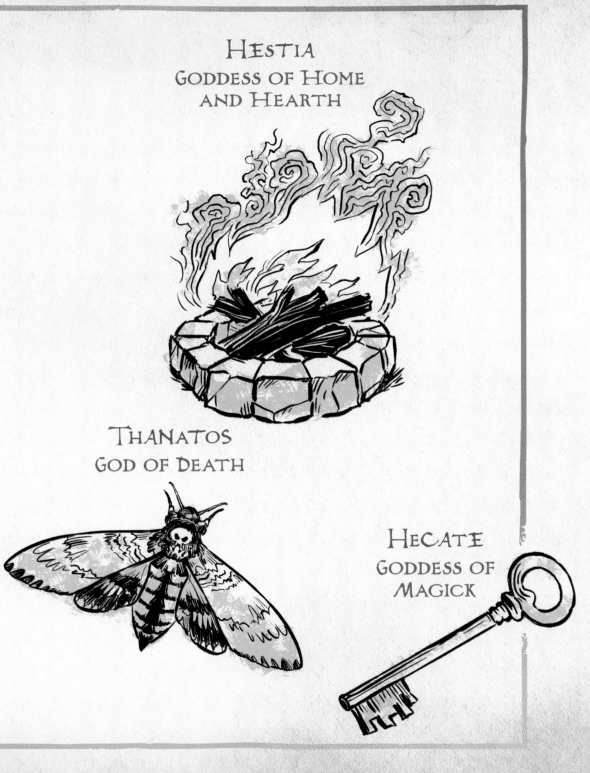

Hestia
Goddess of Home and Hearth

Thanatos
God of Death

Hecate
Goddess of Magick

Invocations to the Beyond

Invocations issue from the lips, a humming drone, a resonating mumble, to call upon supreme forces unseen, to invoke the otherworldly energies to magnify thy magick.

Recite the incantations in guttural warbles, with purring zeal, with impassioned plea.

If they do answer and happen to cross the threshold, ask of them this:

GRANT MY DEEP WISH, O GREAT ONES!

18th of September 1671
We cannot seem to get Sister Sarah to stop chanting throughout the house. . . .

'Tis a gift! 'Tis a gift! 'Tis a gift!

'Tis a headache.

Dionysus Invocation

DIONYSUS, god of grape,

Bacchus, I invoke thee,

Instead of the pouring from thy goblet . . .

Dry up the well

Like the dusty cellar

Like the parched lips

Oh, fruitful god,

Siphon the water

Let the bucket rise with ash and

Wreath of ven'mous ivy

And come to a grinding halt.

A most excellent idea, sister. Tis a desirable dry spell.

Might I recommend using this on the suspecting townsfolk?

Nemesis Invocation

NEMESIS, daughter of Erebus,

Goddess of retribution,

Guided by griffins and justice . . .

I call upon thee: tip the scales

To plague my neighbor with

Endless misfortune and blight

Righter of wrongs, topple my victim

Like the sword balancing on its point

Like the bridle loos'ning from the grip

The crack of thy scourge, and all turneth fair

Rock the scales, hear now my prayer.

It worked on a town elder's little daughters.

I have not lost my touch!

Eos Invocation*

EOS, Aurora, hear my plea,
Goddess of the dawn,
Sister of Helios and Selene;
Thy dawn-chariot turning,
Instead of painting the sky pink . . .
Thy wingéd horses diving to
Cast thy light upon me
Bring the bloom of morning
Into my cheeks, a rosy red that
Brighteneth mine eyes
Like thy tiara of gold
Like thy rosy fingers
Eos, let my visage gleam, and
Bathe me in the red-hued rise.

I want to be wildly charming again!

* *Aha! An invocation that brought the natural rouge back to my cheeks! It won't make me any younger, but it's a start!*

124

Persephone Invocation

PERSEPHONE, hear me,

Kore, goddess of life and death,

Step from the world of shadow to

Flow'ry earth above: aid my scheme . . .

Rot the crop of my victim at the root,

Let the putrid decay fester and the fetid mould sprout

So the plant may wither to husk and shell

So the shoot may bend and the stalk may snap

Leaf and bud molt, they plummet like hope

Burst the pomegranate seeds in their chambers

For this base plot I invoke thee.

Eris Invocation

ERIS, goddess of chaos and strife,

Discordia, daughter of Nyx,

Spurrer of unease and disquiet,

Instead of serving the golden apple of discord . . .

I call upon thee to turn the stomach of my victim

Like the storm-tossed sea of Pandemonium

Like the sloshing barrel of unruliness

The sickly sheen of tumult

The indisposed green of dissent

Make my victim qualmish and

Squirm like the fussing worm.

Sister, get thy nose out of my precious book!

Oops.

Hebe Invocation

Hebe, goddess of youth,

Juventas, daughter of Hera,

I invoke thee to fly down to me like the eagle . . .

For thy nectar and ambrosia, I plea

Grow my tresses,

Slather them with honeyed varnish

Let the strands lengthen

Let the locks loosen and extend

So that I may look young again

Hear my lament so that my hair

May grow to touch the earth.

I think it worked, Winnie! But while my hair grew longer, its texture keepeth switching from straight to curly!

Thou agest me, sister.

Thanatos Invocation

Hear me, O god of doom,

Brother of Hypnos and the Keres

Bearing sword of shadow'd steel,

I pray thou dost hollow the egg

Of my victim's sleeping chicken

Let the shell stay whole

Let the egg keep dense

But with the cracking, the empty promise within,

This most trivial trick, a most delectable surprise

O mighty THANATOS, regard my fervent hope

And execute thy destructive controul.

Hestia Invocation

HESTIA, goddess of hearth,

Thy flames and fire,

Instead of protecting mine home . . .

I invoke thee to clean mine cauldron

Remove stain and smear

Remove aged mark

Allow my pot to shine

Like the obsidian boulder

Like the gleaming bubble

Let cogent remnants wash away

So new draughts can be unsullied.

I would rather let Mary keep dealing with this chore the old-fashioned way—with grit.

Helios Invocation

HELIOS, hear me,

Helius, god of sun,

Thy chariot landing

Instead of soaring forth to steal the stars . . .

On Pyrois, on Aeos, on Aethon, on Phlegon

Hooves touch down in dust

Scorching the earth

Like the scalding sun-rays

Like the blistering diadem

Let thine energy shine upon me

So that I may radiate thy light.

Hecate Invocation

I beg thee, O Great HECATE, direct

Thy fiery majesty towards me;

And impart in this staff

The power of yore.

Let thy strength entwine with the wood

Like two strings braided into one

Let thy magick rest within each splinter

Biding, halting, pulsing

Like a cat waiting to jump its prey

So that I may wield thine energy

With most precision and might.

Where is the invocation to turn
mine bodice from green to purple?
Or purple to green?

Creatures of the Beyond

Creatures of the Beyond dwell in lakes and forests, on craggy mountaintops. They are beings most fearsome and monstrous, wielding power not bound to the natural world. They know only a hunger that cannot be satiated.

Hobgoblins, hobgoblins, all in a row,
Eat all the candy so that you grow!
Hobgoblins, hobgoblins, towering tall,
Please do not eat me now I'm very small!

Oh, cheese and crust!
I had forgotten about
such hideous beasts.

Don't remember, Winnie!
Don't remember!

Brimstone Viper

An enormous reptile with unholy design
of both snake and bird that guardeth
the gates of the Beyond and breatheth
fire and brimstone at all who dare try
to flee the under-world. The beast hath
three emerald-flamed heads that sprout
from a pale body covered in oozing scales.
It speweth potent venom at its victims,
coating them in a diaphanous web, before
smiting them with a single scorching gaze.
The Brimstone Viper should never be
startled. Those who can master stealth may
be able to circumvent its sulf'rous coils.

I can charm a snake with my voice!

Plague-ridden beast!

*The brimstone viper
is just misunderstood!*

Vile Fish

Apparently, the fish rots from the head down?

Ravenous fish that prey on those who would dare to walk the shores or voyage the pitch'd waters of the Styx, Lethe, Acheron, Phlegethon, or Cocytus. Black cattle who stray from Menoetes' herd will meet a shallow fate. The Vile Fish strip away all till only bone remaineth and the Keres swarm the remaining foam. The creatures possess the finned body of fish, the point'd fangs of the Lamiae, the red eyes of the Mormolyceia, and assume the faces of those consumed, be it cow, dog, sheep, or unlucky witch.

'Tis a good thing I cannot swim, sisters!

I need to remember that next time thou disturbs my peace, Sister. The creek and churning waterwheel are but a stone's toss away. . . .

Get her, Winnie!

Dire Worm

A tiny worm said to be clipped from
Medusa's scalp that lurketh within the
pores of rocks and cheweth through
the orchards tended by the jaundiced
Ascalaphus. The worm stayeth quiet and
hidden, and draweth blood from unwitting
ankles. The Dire Worm gorgeth itself
until it groweth to reach insurmountable
heights. Most revered and feared, the
worm's screech is cause for Melinoe to
haunt the living, for the Cacodaemones to
take refuge, and for the winged Thanatos
to wield his protective blade. Once the
Dire Worm beginneth to constrict a body,
its embrace marketh the last.

They make for good snacks when still young!

Imps!
Every last one of them!

The Dead

ON THE DEAD AMONGST THE
LIVING, FOR THY CONTROLLING
AND THY GRASPING,

The Dead are never really gone.
Sometimes, the Dead are found
wandering the Beyond. . . .

Sometimes, the Dead can return to
thee in the Realm of the Living. . . .

Maggot museums!

But if I could
command them
to do my bidding . . .

A Dance of the Dead

Reaching the Dead

The Dead from beyond the gates of the under-world can be brought back to walk among the Realm of the Living, reached with words and whispers, these vap'rous wisps used to do thine unseemly biddings. . . .

To bring about the Plague of Darkness, recite the incantation thrice:

Pestis
Tenebrarum
Locusta
Vomicaque

Nothing makes me happier.
That is, when the icy breath
of death comes for another!

Communicating with the Dead

To correspond with the Dead, utterance
of the nine sacred and magickal names:

YAGA ✦ GOWDIE ✦ SOUTHEIL ✦ SHIPTON ✦ FORTUNE ✦ MORGAN ✦ KYTELER ✦ SAMPSON ✦ VOISIN

ALLOW THE EARS
OF ALL THE REST TO
HEAR MY VOICE, AND
FOR THE ONE I CALL
TO ANSWER.

Secrets of the Grave

On All Hallows' Eve, the spirits of the Dead can move among the living. To call upon a spirit on Hallows' Eve, recite this incantation:

SPIRIT, HEAR ME . . .

DASH THE NIGHT IN THE GLOW
OF THY SPECTRAL FORM,

LUCID NOW THOU ART A FEARFUL SIGHT.

TRANSLUCENT SOUL, ROAM WHEREVER
THOU PLEASEST

TRAVERSE TO EARTH'S REMOTEST
BOUNDS, OR NEAR AT HAND;

WITH SHINING INCENSE, I CALL THEE
FORTH, UNAFRAID

TO ONCE MORE CROSS INTO MY
REALM WITH RITES DIVINE.

Winnie, I am afraid of ghosts!

Boo!

Summoning from Beyond the Veil

To bring forth one's spirit in corporeal form so it may walk amongst man in flesh once more until the rise of the sun, say these words on Hallows' Eve:

UNTRUTHFUL
SOUL DEEP
IN THY TOMB,

ASLEEP LIKE THE
BABE IN THE WOMB.

STRETCH THY LIMBS,
ROLL OPEN THINE EYES,

WHAT ONCE WAS STIFF
SHALL BE NOW SPRY.

FALL IN STEP,
BE NOT STILL,

STAND TO
SERVE MY
WICKED
WILL.

A most intriguing spell . . .

Using Specters as Doubles

Through the permeable veil, the creeping specter
The assumption of the translucent form, a double
The floating through muddy road unsullied
The visiting of mortals unbeknownst
Thou swimmest through the troubled air, unseen,
Succeeding chore and task before the return
To the body long since left behind.

I was able
to become a ghost
for but a day and
pinch the pie
off the baker's sill!

Evil Hand

With bevy of specters at thy command,
Prick and pinch through another's ghostly hand
Meddle with matters without a ripple,
With aid of coven, effort doth triple.

1st of May 1674
The town elders are suspicious of our
~pinching and pricking. sisters!

Blast them! We must take precaution,
or they will burn us at the stake, or worse!

Save us, Winnie! Save us!

Bitter Things

As specter for a brief time, peek and peer in places otherwise forbidden . . . the Bitter Things . . .
Use bodies of water to spy on thy victims, as they wash their faces in basin, as they lead their horses to trough, as they talk in hushed voices over dirty puddles with the semblance of retreat.

To control the ability to spy on the Bitter Things, recite the incantation once:

SALEM
SUB MARI

A meddlesome little child escaped our clutches!
The townsfolk seem to be getting better at protecting their young.

Ghostly Voice

In the form of a temporary specter, thou hast the ability to throw thy voice so that victims afar wake to hear it 'neath bed, in cupboard, down darkly descending stairs. In this way, thou canst whisper thine inclinations to best sway steadfast fools, frighten victims past the brink of sleepless frenzy into delirium and hysteria, and converse with coven from distant shores. . . .

To exercise the Ghostly Voice, recite the incantation thrice:

TRUX SUBRIDENS LARVA

Magick of the Red Witch

N THE MAGICK OF POTIONS AND SPELLS, FOR THY VITRIOL AND THY VINDICATING,

After practices and preparations, thou canst now try thine hand at deeper magick, magick of potion making for vengeance, rituals for perseverance, divination for thy knowing, and delving into dreams to meddle and muddle. Use thy voice and heav'nly gestures to chant for good fortune, to hex for punishing, to curse for malevolence, to spell for success, to sing for trickery and control. Go forth, and let the text on these pages seep into thy being.

Rituals of Resolution

ON THE RITUALS AND WITCHY PRACTICES TO EMBOLDEN THY RESOLVE AND THY SPIRIT.

To rededicate thyself to thy noble craft and secret life with the sanctified rituals . . .   *I rededicate myself to my craft.*

Rituals of Fire & Brimstone

Thou must pledge to stride onward on this winding and treach'rous path. Thy power will grow, thy destiny will be fulfilled:

WITCHING HOUR

The coven joineth hands beneath full moon to lament the day, to be purged of nagging thoughts.

ETERNAL PATH

The coven gathereth to renew the promised vow of the dedication to the eternal path of witchcraft.

SHADOW OF MOON

The coven cometh together to rest without the practice of magick, to reconnect with guiding moon.

Develop thine own habits to sharpen thy skills, to intensify thy magick on thine upward route.

Angering Circle

When anguish brimmeth into madness,
Lodged in heart of racing badness,
Form a circle, hand in hand in hand,
Deepen thine anger till 'tis fanned,
Rage to channel and charge,
To blast once it grows large.

Perhaps we might consider discontinuing this practice, Sister Winnie? Sister Winnie is very angry!

Why, I have no need for this fulsome practice.

Calming Circle

When night turneth dire and all seemeth lost,

Rouse soothing thoughts at any cost,

Form a circle, hand in hand in hand,

Make inner din wane, small from grand,

    Serenity and peace,

      My unrest now can cease.

Soothing Thoughts:

- *Rabid Dogs*
- *Black Death*
- *Mummy's Scorpion Tartlet*

I have an idea! Perhaps we could all form this calming circle more often . . . ?

No need!

And if thou suggestest this one more time,
I shall have your guts for garters, girl!

Dark Divination

ON THE DARK DIVINATION OF WITCHES, FOR THY GAZING AND THY GLIMPSING,

To see into the present, to gaze into the past, to glimpse into the future, practice of the three mystic methods:

OOMANCY   TASSEOMANCY   PALMISTRY

Artifacts of Clairvoyance

SCRYING MIRROR OF ENCHANTRESS THORN

ORACLE ORB OF THE WATER WITCH

CRYSTAL SPHERE OF HELENA

I have yet to master scrying. My current aging reflection is but a hideous distraction.

Oomancy

Crack egg into glass, and decipher the dancing shapes of the whites.

Yolk breaking spells doom.
Double yolk spells doom.
Blood spot spells doom.

Doom, *doom,* and more **doom!**
'Tis more doom
than I can bear.

Perhaps we shall not put all our eggs in one fiery handbasket, Sister?

Tasseomancy

Ode to oracles of long ago, seeking truth
Three sisters, goddesses of destiny *Is this us?!*
Of the Master guiding mediations.
Drink sour tea and scour patterns of the acrid leaves
Interpret symbols, and discover the meaning therein.

SYMBOLS & MEANINGS

BLOOD MOON—Melancholy

CHEESE & CRUST—Death
Uh-oh. I got this one. Wiiiiinnie!

*Fare thee well, Dear Sister.
I shall miss thy comforting hold.*

WITCH'S MARK—Protection

MAGGOTY MALFEASANCE—Prosperity

HOCUS POCUS—Distraction

*My tea leaf formed
this sha—O! A shiny thing!* *Distracted dolt!*

Hocus Pocus

Palmistry

Foresee thy character on thy palm
And foretell what fortune
Lieth underneath thy skin
Read lines of fate, moon, witch,
Magick, power, and death
So thou might behold the knowledge to
Take fate into thine own hands.

1) FATE LINE

2) MOON LINE

3) WITCH LINE

4) MAGICK LINE

5) POWER LINE

6) DEATH LINE

Sisters! I have read my fate line.
Life is but a bowl of chokecherries!

Steeped in Dreaming

On the Fragile Dreams and Nightmares, for Thy Deranging and Thy Distorting,

Through powers of Oneiros, thou hast the ability to visit dreams, to manipulate the wills of many, to trick and deceive. Recite these passages to control thy victim's sleeping thought. . . .

The Fulfilling Dream

I grant thee the gift of flight without a broom,
A future foretold in the light of the moon
Rejoined are lost ones
With radiance of suns
Awaken healed and feeling
newly hewn.

Ahh, a beauty sleep.
How I had hoped it would work to bring me
back to the bloom of my youth. Dashed!

The Haunting Nightmares

Nightmare cloaked in thistledown, quilt, and candle,
The sunset fadeth, and thou fallest from craggy cliff
Runnest from maddened mass
Bangest on sarcophagus
Arisest with brow beaded and
shoulders stiff.

The Manipulating Dreams & Nightmares

I alight upon thy dream to twist with bane,

Controlling the course of thy still-dormant thoughts

Old is now turned new

Sky is green, grass is blue

When thou wakest, thy mind's morphed

to tie my knots.

I could make the children dream of following me

and sleepwalk through the sweet woods!

Now if only I could make my crushes dream of me...

Chants of Yore

ON THE OLDE SACRED CHANTS OF WITCHES, FOR THY MANIFESTING AND THY PROTECTING,

Recite the chants of yore to connect
thyself to power of mind, body, and spirit,
and call forth thy magick most desired. . . .

Chant of Remembrance

REMEMBER, REMEMBER,
THE FIRE, THE EMBER;

REMEMBER, REMEMBER,
LEAVES DROP IN SEPTEMBER;

REMEMBER, REMEMBER
THE COVEN, EACH MEMBER;

REMEMBER, REMEMBER,
FROSTS BITE IN NOVEMBER;

REMEMBER, REMEMBER,
SNOWS FALL IN DECEMBER;

REMEMBER, REMEMBER,
THE FIRE, THE EMBER.

Sister Winnie, thou must remember to use this one more often. 'Tis good for finding lost items.

It worked! I lost my lucky rat tail again, but remembered it was right where I left it!

I need to remember to stop letting you two thundering lubberworts write in my darling book.

Chant to Tarnish Mirror

Make the mirror much
less clearer:

REFLECTION
DEFLECTION

COMPLEXION
REJECTION

PERFECTION
EJECTION

PROTECTION
INFECTION

AFFECTION
ABJECTION

To undo, wave hands
over mirror's surface,
and recite thrice:

DIRECTION
CORRECTION

Why would anyone do such a terrible thing?!

Chant to Spoil Butter & Milk

I would not want to be on the receiving end of this chant!

BEFORE THE DUNK
TO SLIPP'RY CHUNK;
THE FUST OF FEET
TO TURN THE SWEET;
THE SCREAM OF STEAM
TO CURD THE CREAM;
THE CHURNING SCHEME,
TO SPURN THE DREAM.

'Tis worse than a spoiled appetite!

Chant to Make Cow Sick

Who would do such a cruel thing to a nice little cow, Winnie?

Me.

BOVINE MALIGN
BOVINE RESIGN
BOVINE RECLINE
BOVINE CONFINE
BOVINE ENTWINE

Followed
by the utterance:

U
UT
UTT
UTTE
UTTER
UDDER
UDDERA
UDDERAN
UDDERANC
UDDERANCE

Chant to Smell Children

I SMELL A CHILD
TENDER AND MILD;

I SMELL A CHILD
PLUMP AND BEGUILED;

I SMELL A CHILD
WINDY AND WILD;

I SMELL A CHILD
THEIR FEARS EXILED.

My power! My nose always knows when it smells a child! I think this chant appears to make my sense even stronger, though my nostrils tingle and are actually really starting to burn. . . .

Chant to Cause Infestation

'NEATH RAFTER
AND TIDY EAVE,

RATS' NEST I DO
DARKLY WEAVE.

BUGS AND MICE
BEGIN TO PEEVE,

QUIETNESS GONE
ENOUGH TO GRIEVE.

THY WALL A SLOW-
WRITHING SLEEVE,

THY CEILING DOTH
SAG AND HEAVE.

THY FLOORBOARDS
BEGIN TO SKIVE,

THE PEACE I DO
WICKEDLY THIEVE,

LEST WARY
OCCUPANTS LEAVE.

*Infestations make for a bounty of lucky
rat tails just waiting to be gnawed!*

Chant to Make Socks Itchy

POISON IVY AND
A FIRE ANT

INSIDE THE SOCK AND
LINED IN THE PANT

LET PRICKLING SEND
TO A SCRATCHING
TRANCE

TRAPPED IN THE
SEALED BOOT,
A THRASHING DANCE

AGONIZING JERK,
THE DEED IS DONE

STOCKING TO
TORMENT AND SOCK
TO STUN.

A chant I shall attempt
to invoke on my
ungrateful sister Sarah,
that rotter!

Persistent Potions

ON THE POTENT POTIONS OF WITCHES, FOR THY LIPS, OR THOSE OF THY VICTIM,

Whether stirring a draught to transform mermaid to human, or immortal to mortal . . .

Love Potion

FOR CREATING AMOR

When love unrequited needeth but a nudge:

With the incantation of Aphrodite, with the petals of red rose, with the oil of saffron blessed under a full moon, with the stem of foxglove, with the gaunt lily.

Bring to a roiling bubble, then add three leaves of jewelweed, and hearts of palm.

When the potion is done, pour in hollow'd pomegranate, and allow to sleep for nine days and nine nights. When 'tis complete, gift it to the person whose love thou seekest. After they drink it, stand in front of them and recite thrice:

I HAVE MADE THEE CRAVE.

It was love at first bite!
Now if we could just tie the knots . . .

~~Winnie~~ + Billy
Sarah

Formula of Solace

FOR EASING TENSIONS

When clouded mind droneth with scorning thoughts of Moros and Momus:

With the essence of nightshade, with the sprig of catnip, with the petal of violet, with the seed of vervain, with the bark of hawthorn,

With the bead of amber which hath been given for tempering

Bring to a simmer, then add five leaves of chickweed.

When the potion is done, add the drop of anise oil, then anoint thyself and recite thrice: *The magick words!*

I HAVE MADE MY DAUNTED THOUGHTS CALM.

All those cursèd sisters of mine seem to brew up is a ruckus!

Levitation Potion

FOR LIFTING OBJECTS

When object is beyond thy reach and thou
needest it glide into thy grasp:

     1 PART WEB OF SPIDER *Ah! A darling spider!*

     1 PART CLUMP OF LICHEN

     2 PARTS PAD OF LILY

     1 PART WING OF WASP

     4 PARTS DILL

     3 PARTS KNOTWEED

     1 PART LAUREL

     2 PARTS TURNIP

     1 PART GOLDENSEAL OIL

Crush and combine them in cauldron hot.
Dab the potion on thine hand, then recite thrice:

AWAKE AND FLOAT!
TAKE TO THE AIR!
RETURN HOME
TO MY TABLE AND CHAIR!

*With a finger snap, my beloved book floats
and flips through the air to me!*

BoOooOook!

Befuddling Potion

FOR CAUSING CONFUSION

When thou wishest to encircle the mind of thy victim in stinging nettles:

3 PARTS SAGE

2 PARTS LEECH

2 PARTS WORMWOOD

1 PART FORGET-ME-NOT

1 PART BRAIN OF NEWT

2 PARTS ROSEMARY

1 PART BUCKTHORN OIL

2 PARTS EXTRACT OF LLAMA

Blend them in cauldron until billowing black smoke doth appear, then let sit for one day and one night and recite once:

THOUGHTS ONCE DAGGER-SHARP SLUICE AND SLOUGH AWAY
THY MIND IS THICKETED, THOU ART MY PREY.

I attempted to use this potion on the town elders to trick them into thinking we are but kindly spinster ladies.

I am not sure it is working. . . . Trouble is brewing! Winnie, try again, O brilliant sister!

I am confused!

Sleeping Draught

FOR BRINGING REST

When stalking thoughts aflame keep eyes ajar:

With the tincture of chamomile, with the berries of holly, with the petal of iris, with the root of valerian, with the leaf of tarragon, with slime of slug and snail, with trefoil and crust of eye,

With the skin of poison apple which hath been given for drowsing, for croaking,

When potion slosheth and spitteth, then add splinter of spinning wheel, rose from the briar, thorn from the thicket, and raven's feather oil. Extinguish flame, and allow to stand for one full night. Recite thrice:

I HAVE PLUNGED THEE INTO UNYIELDING LABYRINTH WITH THE POPPIES OF HYPNOS.

I had a dream that Winnie loved me.

Potion of Bodily Stillness

FOR STOPPING MOTION

When thy limbs quake and flare in times of greatest strain:

With the spore of black mould, with the leaf of woodruff, with the essence of rockrose, with the seed of hemlock, with the foot of june bug, with the skull of shrew, with the pit of withered drupe, with the root of lady's mantle, with caraway and jicama.

Ugh! That vile word again!

With the Seed of Doubt which hath been given for curing twitching spasm,

Once potion shimmereth translucent, add a quill of porcupine. Then ladle ample amount into glass vial with stopper, and allow to sit for sixteen days and fifteen nights. Before taking, recite thrice:

I HAVE BESTILLED MINE HAND
AND BESMIRCHED MINE UNEASE.

Potion of Deception

For Creating a Disguise

When deceiving with lum'nous design or Apate's hunched black rag:

1 Part BLACK OF NIGHT

3 PARTS WITCH'S CACKLE

1 PART SCREAM OF FEAR

2 PARTS MUMMY DUST

1 PART HEART OF PIG

1 PART NETTLE

4 PARTS SHED SNAKESKIN

2 PARTS HAGGARD THYME

1 PART POWDERED SEASHELL

4 PARTS EYE OF NEWT

Mash with mortar and pestle and add to cauldron. When potion fizzeth and glisteneth a bilious green, add a witchetty grub, then recite once:

BEGIN NOW MY MAGICK SPELL, APPEAR MY SECRET JOKE, CHANGE MY WITCHY RAIMENT INTO ANOTHER'S CLOAK!

I pretended I was Winnie when she was off on a particularly long flight.

Me too! Billy could not even tell. I nearly tickled him to death!

Dwindling Potion
For Making One Small

When thou needest to scrabble through doors no higher than a hare:

4 Parts Dried Leaf of Coriander

1 Part Feather of Flamingo

1 Part White Hair of Hare

3 Parts Pus of Pimple

2 Parts Botfly Wing

1 Part Mushroom

2 Parts Myrrh

2 Parts Bluet

1 Part Nit

Sister Mary has plenty of pimples on her back!

Add them in cauldron warm. Wait till mixture firmeth into tiny cakes, then pour liquid remnant into bottle. Cork to stop, and recite thrice:

The Looking Glass Reflects
the Form Now Diminished!

Reversal of Potion
FOR MAKING ONE BIG AGAIN

Only the tiny cake can undo the effect of thy potion.

Healing Draught

FOR RESTORING HEALTH AND YOUTH

When sick and injured pallor of Geras gnaws at long-lost luster:

With the oil of elder flower, with the larva of praying mantis, with the bud of skullcap, with the tincture of tansy, with the sprig of basil, with the blade of fireweed, with the sweat of poison ivy, with the seed of juniper, with the dew of narcissus, with the root of saffron and wood sorrel

With the golden flower which hath been given for the softening, once potion gleameth and gloweth gold, wave thine hands o'er the cauldron, and recite once:

POTION, GLIMMER AND GLISTEN AND SHINE
BRING BACK MINE LIFE-FORCE DIVINE.

Beauty is but skin deep.

17th of August 1682

Sisters! I have lost my youthful glow over the years! Oh, it's just awful! This draught worked for only a fortnight before the wretched wrinkles reappeared! I must try another way to restore myself to a more youthful form. But how . . . ?

Thou dost not need any draught, Sister.

Thou art still a mere sprig of a girl!

Blemish-Giving Potion

FOR CONJURING IMPERFECTIONS

When thy victim lacks warts upon the flawless visage:

With the hound's-tongue, with the wart of hog, with the drop from the Sea of Grief, with the bark of alder, with the oil of walnut and turmeric, with the dust of evening primrose, with the seed of lupine, with the juice of prune, with the oil of nutmeg and castor.

With the rimpled gizzard of turkey which hath been given for the rumpling, the crimping,

Once potion shimmereth with dappled pearlescence, add a silkworm and a barberry. Then mix the brew with ochre black, squeeze a single drop onto thy victim's face, and recite thrice:

A SPELL OF SPITE TO RUCK VELLUM FAIR
GIVE MY VICTIM A FACE TO SCARE.

There is nothing worse than a putrid, festering sore on thy face.

Potion of Dishonesty

For Making Others Believe Thy Lies

When deceit burroweth deep 'neath peat and loam:

3 Parts oil of Licorice Root
1 Part Lilac
8 Parts Hair of Tarantula
1 Part Viper Heart
1 Part Pearl of Wisdom
4 Parts Echinacea
2 Parts Goiter of Swine
2 Parts Cobra Ruby

I ♡ eating spiders!

Perhaps we can trick the town elders to stop thinking us lying jezebels!

Mix them and add to cauldron. Once potion coalesceth into milky pink, 'tis time. Add a rotten molar of goat. Then recite once:

Trust in dust, believe thou must:
Wind doth wave and waters gust.

Strength Potion

FOR BESTOWING BRAWN

When corporal resolve doth waver and creaking bones protest:

3 PARTS COCKROACH

1 PART BLOOD SAUSAGE

4 PARTS IRONWEED

4 PARTS SNAPDRAGON

1 PART WILLOW SEED

1 PART CROCODILE JAW

5 PARTS YELLOWJACKET

2 PARTS TUSK OF BOAR

1 PART ARM OF ANT

Crumble them and dump in cauldron. Stir sevenfold.
When potion emitteth sulf'rous odor, add hiss of tortoise,
then drain into a goblet and drink, and after recite thrice:

THE WEIGHT I WIELD LIKE ANT UPHILL

WITH STONE ON BACK AND NEVER STILL.

A dose of this potion seemeth to have strengthened me, but now
I am perhaps too strong! I went to fling an ingredient
into the cauldron and it flew right over it and straight
through the wall!

I blame Mary!

Sorry, Winnie! Wouldst thou like to jab me?

Flight Potion

How is this different from the Levitation Potion?

FOR BESTOWING FLIGHT

When ground draweth thee down in slow strides of muck and molasses:

Without the hefty rock, without the pull of earth

With the featherweight, with the floating of feet, with the sheer rising, with the agile gliding, with the buoyant jaunting, with the graceful swooping, with the airy stream through wood and cloud

With the seed of mustard, with the seed of chokecherry and hyssop, with the clipping of agrimony, with the oil of mugwort, with the sedge of fern, with the feather of raven, with the powder of moth, with the dust of Minthe, with the whirl of dandelion

With the will o' the wisp which hath been given for the nimble hov'ring,

Add them to cauldron until potion breatheth a swimming white cloud. Then anoint thy broom, and recite once:

COME! I FLY! FROM PATH OF
DIRT TO PATH OF SKY!

Life Potion

For Restoring Thy Youth

When time carveth lines, and the cruel end doth threaten:

Begin by taking a child young and supple, tender and pretty, then continue with the potion:

With the slime of hagfish, with the powder of rue, with the drop of rosewater, with the dash of pox, with the dab of saliva of newt, with the two drops of oil of boil, with the dead man's toe.

Add them to cauldron, and stir thrice. Contents should form a purple-pink mist.

With piece of thine own tongue which hath been given for the ebbing,

Bring to a hissing green simmer, then pour down the child's gullet. Observe, for when the skin of the child flareth with a life-force most misty, breathe in the gleaming essence, and thou shalt be young and spry once more.

CHILD, VICTIM, OUR HOLIEST GRAIL,
THY GLOWING AURA WE SHALL INHALE.

This!
This may just do the trick!

Fulsome Hexes, Curses & Spells

ON THE SACRED SPELLS OF WITCHES, FOR THY CURSING AND HEXING HAND,

Thou hast learned many ways of the witch, but none are so powerful as the sacred spells, the hankering hexes, the cruelest curses. These spells require a heightened level of focus and growth.

Let thine intention clear, and let thy words build and swell with the weight of thy darkest wish.

12th of May 1685
'Tis impressive Winnie can memorize so many spells!

Apparently, Sister Winnie hath difficulty committing potion recipes to memory.

Remember, Winnie! Remember!

Shut your yaps!
Sister Sarah cannot spell or spell!

Bitter Hexes

The most vile punishment taketh the shape of the spell.
Turning thy victim into a wooden puppet . . . A terrible
horned beast . . . A candlestick or a carpet . . . Stealing thy
victim's voice and assuming their corporal form . . . Inducing
an endless sleep with the prick of a single finger . . .
The most foul spell can also come in the hiss of the tiniest
hex. The best hex starteth small and groweth like a hook
of ivy creeping 'cross the trellis till 'tis all-consuming. . . .
Maladies . . . Ailments . . . Afflictions . . .

Aha! My most
dangerous spells!
They have a
wonderful way
of lingering, I've
found. . . .

Winnie, wouldst
thou like to hex me
if it maketh thee
feel better?

Bitter Hexes

 ABSCESS
ACHES
ACNE

 BEDBUGS
BRONCHITIS
BLISTERS *Burning Rash* *Burping!*

 CACKLING COUGH
CAVITY   *Winnie practiced on me. and it worked!*
CYST   *I have since filled the rot with gold.*

Creaking Bones. **The horror!**

 DIZZINESS
DROOPING
DRY MOUTH

Bitter Hexes

Earache
Eye Infection
Eyelash Crust *Eyesores. the two of you.*

Fever
Fleas *Filth*
Flu

Gas
Gizzard *Ugh!*
Gum Recession

Hay Fever *Hackles! Haunches! Hooves!*
Head Lice
Hookworm

Bitter Hexes

ILLUSIONS
IMPETIGO
INSOMNIA *Irritable Bowel Syndrome*

JAMMED TOE
JIGGLING ENDLESSLY
JITTERS **Joint Pain**

KEELING OVER
KIDNEY STONES
KNUCKLE PUS

LETHARGY *Laryngitis! Perhaps, Sister*
LEG CRAMPING *Sarah, thou needest to work*
LIVER SPOTS *on the placement of thy*
voice when singing songs to
ensure healthy cords . . . ?

Bitter Hexes

 MIGRAINE
MUMPS
MUSCLE ACHES

 NAIL FUNGUS
NAUSEA
NOSEBLEED *This would be very bad for me.*

 OOZING EYEBALLS
OUTBREAK OF BOILS
OVERFLOWING BLADDER

 PETRIFICATION *Parched Throat!*
POLYPS
PATCH OF POX *Poison used to silence unfaithful lovers!*

Bitter Hexes

 Quacking Loudly
Quelling
Quiver and Quake

 Rancor
relentless Humming
Runny nose

 Scarlet Fever
Shingles
Sneezing Fits *Spider Veins*

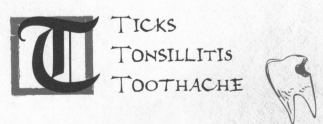 Ticks
Tonsillitis
Toothache

Bitter Hexes

Hath Winnie hexed Mary? She hath been burping for many a moon!

 UPSET STOMACH
UNRAVELING INTESTINES
UGLINESS

 VENOM
VEXATION
VOMIT

 WEAKNESS
WHIPWORM
WRINKLES *The worst hex of them all.*

 XANTHOMA
XEROPHTHALMIA
XYLOPHAGIA

Bitter Hexes

 Yak Breath
Yawning Infinitely
Yeast of the Neck *Yelping*

 Zapped Energy
Zigzagging Steps
Zombie Stitches

What an intriguing idea . . .

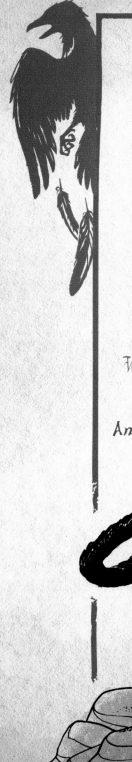

Unsavory Curses

Curses! What a treat.

And now for blasphemous punishments most brutish, whose forsaken magick wieldeth greater lasting effect than a Fulsome Hex, whose devious casting invoketh Arae and requireth a stronger degree of thy magick: Unsavory Curses . . .

May these insuff'rable curses work to transform thy victim into a frog or bear, or worse. . . .

Winnie hath the curse of always being right.
          And she's always cursing me under her breath.
And I have the curse of having two thundering oafs for sisters!

Curse of Eternal Dancing

Bewitch thy victims into dancing eternally until their demise;

The limbs will flail and shimmy, an uncontrollable writhing that will continue, on and on and on, with or without a tune to inspire. Side to side, feet will tire. Side to side, muscles will give way. Side to side, the body will sway. There is no stillness.

The Command

NOCTE SALTA TOTA
DIE SALTA TOTO
SALTA AETERNALITER
DUM NON POSSIS
SALTARE SALTA

Oh, this curse soundeth like a most
joyous blessing, sisters! I love to dance and prance!

This curse worked wonders
at the town council meeting
we crashed. . . .

Curse of Swine

When visitor steppeth foot past thy threshold and thou wishest them stay

Change them into something to ensure they remain more than a day.

With bristles, spots, warts, and hooves, with squeals and oinking, the snorting, snuffling swine cannot run far when trapped in thy sty. And over time, it shall forget who it once was, and succumb to remaining thy pet, with its only joys the rolling in the mud, the squelch of thy step.

The Command

MUTA CIRCE HOMINEM IN SUEM
ET SUS VIVAT IN SORDIDA HARA
ET SUS NUMQUAM EGREDIATUR EX INSULA

We love when Winnie turneth meddlesome souls into animals!

Yes! We never know which beast Winnie is going to pick!

Why, thank you sisters. Now behave, or you shall be next up!

Curse of Wolf

The night, full moon, giveth white fur. The howl, guttural hunger. The change with each watchful Mother Moon.

May this curse last for an eternity of prowling, with just the panting tread. Lone wolf, padding the corners of ev'ry wood and glen, a solitary fate, a howl that is not met with response. Alone, thy victim taketh to its haunches and crieth.

The Command
BRISTLES AND FUR NOW COAT THE BEING
LUPUS SOLUS GRADITUR
CANINE FANGS AND YELLOW EYES DO STING
LUPUS SOLUS GRADITUR
RELEASE A HOWL AND LET IT RING
LONE-WOLF-HOUND

Curse of Cat

I shall reserve this spell for a most detestable little child.

Transform thy victim into a creature of superstition: the cat. A hissing, bristling bad omen, bound to a body most intolerable. This fulsome punishment lingereth and lasteth like the best of them. For this curse is forever, a lifetime trapped in the feline form. A cruel fate for anyone, a soul strapped to the Everlasting Life.

The Command

CURVE THE BONES WITH ARCH IN SPINE
FI FELES FUSCA PELLIS
BODY WANE WITH MEWLING WHINE
FI FELES FUSCA PELLIS
SPROUT THICK BLACK FUR WITH LIVES NINE
LET-IT-BE

Curse of Dog *Rrrrruff!*

Thou canst not teach old dogs new tricks, as Winnie says!

The less dignified canine, common terrier, with undesirable traits powerless, pathetic, and dependent. The itch cannot be scratched. The fleas, the ticks, the determined burs. May the bark of this curse be worse than its bite. A dog without an owner cannot care for itself.

It beggeth for scraps, and stalketh heels for a lifetime. Its whine deterreth and no one offereth a hand for fear. Heinous, horrible mutt, forever muzzled.

The Command

BARK AND BITE AND BARE THE TEETH
AMICUS OPTIMUS NEMINIS
YIP AND YAP AND YOWL BEQUEATH
AMICUS OPTIMUS NEMINIS
SLEEPING-DOG-WAKE

29th of December 1690

We shall all look as mangy as dogs if we do not make that Life Potion soon. . . .

My Plot to Be Young Again:

1. I shall brew the Life Potion to restore my youth.
2. Sister Mary will sniff out a child.
3. Sister Sarah will lure the child to our abode.
4. I shall use the potion to drain the child of their life-force!

Curse of Llama

Change thy victim into a creature most useless: the llama, a yawning, spitting beast. Reserved for the king most callous. Give the two ears.

Next, the neck, tall and woolly. Then the four hooves, and face with horrid long tooth.

Last, the body, a walking shaggy rug. A fate worse than death.

The Command
CARTILAGE, CRACK, FOR EARS TO EXTEND
LLAMA IMPERATOR NIHIL REGIT
FACE, ELONGATE, FOR TOOTH TO DESCEND
LLAMA IMPERATOR NIHIL REGIT
BODY, BEND, FOR THE CURSE TO DISTEND

NOW-'TIS-DONE

I have learned Sarah has been seeing
my dear Billy in secret!

I would use this curse to bring
forth my revenge, but I do not think it would
be punishment enough. . . .

Protection from Curses

To protect thyself from these punishments, recite the mantra:

PROTECT
THYSELF FROM
PUNISHMENT
GREAT

PROTECT
THINE
HEART

PROTECT
THY
FACE

AND KEEP
THYSELF FREE
OF CURSES
MIGHTY
AND
SMALL

Spells & Spell Preparation

I can spell Boys!
B—O—Y—S!
Boys!

ON THE ARTISTRY OF ONEROUS SPELLS, FOR THY PRACTICING AND THY CASTING,

At long last, the spells, the truest mark of the witch, requiring sageness and most focused magick, the keenest and most fastidious skills . . . All thy practice and toil have led thee here. . . .

Begin with the preparation of candle making to light the way for thy spells. . . .

Ahh!
My most powerful spells at last . . .

Thou art almighty, Winnie!

Process of Preparation

Squeeze the lard of lover long lost into thy cauldron
Add a strand of greasy hair for the wiry wick of the tip
Carve thy symbols and runes into the side of the candle
that carry the essence of thy spell's markéd intention
Call upon the Witches of Yore, and recite thrice:

CANDELA VOLUNTATE MEA FLAMMET

Spell to Travel to the Past

RUBY FLAME CANDLE

When lit by a witch on the night of the
Blood Moon, the candle shineth
to allow the witch to control the
Winds of Change, for but one day.

Recite the words below:

'NEATH HARVEST MOON FAIR
WHEN THE NIGHT IS PRIME
A WITCH WILL WIELD THE AIR
AND TURN BACK THE TIME.
REMEA AD PRAETERITUM
VENTI TEMPORIS

Spell to Drain a Witch of Magick

EMERALD FLAME CANDLE

When lit by a witch on the night of the Moon After Yule, the candle burneth to allow the witch to strip another of their Divine Powers, for but one night.

Recite the words below:

COME MOON OF COLD HOURS

BEFORE YULE AND HAIL

DRAIN A WITCH OF ALL POWERS

TO RENDER THEM FRAIL.

POTENTIAS EXHAURI

MALEFICA IMPOTENS

Those trollimog sisters of mine would not dare attempt this.

Then again, they lack the power to conjure any spell.

We would never, Winnie!

If I am not mistaken, Sister Sarah . . . ?

Spell to Summon Familiars Arcane

Violet Flame Candle

When lit by a witch on the night of the Rotten Egg Moon, the candle sputtereth to allow the witch to summon the Age-Olde Familiars of Yore, for but one day.

Recite the words below:

Egg Moon in the North

Signalleth Summ'ning Stage

Come ancient Familiar Forth

of Witch Wise and Sage.

Animalia Fida Fideles Servi

I wish to summon Mummy's toad!

I hear he was secretly a prince waiting to be kissed!

Spell to Resurrect the Dead

BLACK FLAME CANDLE

Black Flame Candle!

When lit by a virgin on All Hallows' Eve, the candle gloweth to allow witches to come back to life, for but one night.

At sun's first light, ashes to ashes, dust to dust.

Eternal life can be granted if the returning witches can concoct the potion and drain the lives of children.

Recite the words below:

On all Hallows' eve

With the Full MOon Pale

One will Cut thy leave

From beyond the veil.

Voca Mortuos Maleficae Resurgunt

Magician's Spell

To reach witches Beyond the Veil, utter the eleven divine and mystic names:

GUNNILDA ARDEN

ODELINA ARDEN

ISOLDE FITZROU

MATHILDA PICARDY

EVE HARVEY

AMICE HARVEY

FRANCES HARVEY

CECILY SANDERISSON

EMMA SANDERISONE

DRUSCILLA SANDERSON

Doth this mean that I shall be able to talk with Mother again?

Ha! Thou hast fluff where a brain should reside!
We must utter eleven names, yet this list only names ten!

Exchange Spell

I would like to exchange Mary, and with her gone, I'd summon a handsome devil!

Oh, look. Is this not a clever little spell? Though it could spell disaster. . . .

Winnie, I am under thy spell! I live to serve thee!

If thou seekest to bring back a lost one, find a victim in the present and recite this spell to force them to trade places with the desired lost one, even if the lost one writhes in the realms of the Beyond.

The Incantation

SOME INSIDE
AND SOME WITHOUT,

ONE BELIEVES
AND ONE HOLDS
DOUBT.

ON ALL HALLOWS' EVE
'ERE TWELVE
IS STRUCK,

TRADE . . . SOULS
UNTIL SUNUP.

Regurgitating Life Spell *Blech!*

HEREBY I WITH
MOONLIGHT SANCTIFY,
AND HISS UPON THE
TWELVE TABLES . . .

TRICK US, TRAP US,
TRY YE MIGHT,

OUR SPIRITS RETURN
ONE DARK NIGHT:

ALL HALLOWS' EVE,
WHEN THE FLAME
IS LIT:

A FRESH SOUL WILL
BECKON US FROM THE
FIERY PIT.

*I shall see to it my addlebrained sisters stop
dawdling about and gather 'round to memorize this
fascinating incantation. . . . It could prove useful one day. . . .*

I have gladly memorized it for thee, Winnie!

Blazing Inferno Spell

ABLAZE I WITH HADES SUPPLYING,
AND SIC THE BELCHING WORMS AT THEE …

SNAKE UP LATTICE, LICK AT SILL,
THE FOUNDATIONS CRUMBLE AND SPILL:

WOOD TO ASHY HEAP OF SULF'ROUS SMOKE:

I BREATHE IN THE HONEY-SWEET AIR
WHILST OTHERS CHOKE.

I started a fire in the village. It was beautiful!

Unlock-Door Spell

Twice I
With Runnel
Of Bile fashion,

And Agitate the
Dead-Bolted
Doors . . .

Jolt lock,
Wring knob,
Try i might,

Impetuous Efforts
Thwart my plight.

Merciless Filament,
Formed of Mist.

Doors Sealed Tight Will
Open With a Flick of My Wrist.

2nd of June 1692

I wonder if this spell doth work on hearts . . . .

A MOST
Definite, Peculiar, and Real Finding of
VVITCHES.

Being observed by some of the farmers, as they were flying on broom sticks in the upper regions of sky and riding them over the fields and tree tops of Salem Village. Together with the echœs of chanting by the harbor, with the sick milk cow and the afflicted maiden.

Printed by Samuel Parris, 1692.

The blasted townspeople are on to us again, sisters!
We need be more secretive! Curse that Samuel Parris! Curse him!

Why curse him when we can hex his child, Winnie?
'Tis the worst kind of retribution!

We have tried tormenting little Betty Parris, but 'tis not enough!
Let us steal her away!

Jealousy Spell

TWICE I WITH SAGE
JEALOUSY BESMIRCH,
AND LODGE ENVY
WITHIN THINE
HEART ...

EACH LONG SIP I TAKE,
THOU THIRSTEST,
WHILE I FLOURISH AND
BUD, THOU ART CURSED:

ONE JOYOUS DAY,
WHEN I POSSESS ALL:
THOU SHALT FEEL
BEREFT AND
SUCCUMB TO
THY DOWNFALL.

*My dearest Billy
has gone missing!
I hope he returns
soon.*

Foot-Tripping Spell

Once I With Elegance Aerify,
And Traipse Into Thy Steady Field …
Rock Thee, Sway Thee,
Thy Cumbrous Stride,
One Foot Riseth While the
Other Doth Slide.
Obdurate Foot, Defy My Spell Not:
Tangle With the Other Foot and
Fall on the Spot.

Obscurity Spell

THRICE I WITH DOMINION CLARIFY,
AND SEIZE THE BOON OF THE COVEN...
FAZE US, THRILL US, WHAT YE WILL,
THE COVEN SHALL NOT DRINK THY NECTAR-SWILL:
WHILST THOU FADEST TO RUIN,
I SHALL IMPRESS:
A PROMINENT WITCH FAVORED ABOVE
ALL THE REST.

My prattling enemies will meet their doom with this spell.

Stitched-Mouth Spell

Deceptive Friend Poisoned Just,
Hold thee Still Whilst I Stitch Disgust.
Our Secrets Bound ForeverMore,
A Moth-Sealed Mouth to Settle the Score.

Vengeance is Ne'er Loud,
In Silence Thou Hast Bowed.

Thrice I With Strand of
Thread Suture Fast,
And Marry Lower Lip
to Upper...

Call Me, Curse Me,
Mumbles all,
My Wrathful Cord Will
Silence thy Drawl.
Through Drivel and Snivel,
With Moth on Thy Tongue:
Another Untrue Tune
Will Nevermore Be Sung.

I shall cast this spell on that two-timing
Billy Butcherson. That'll keep his
mouth shut, even in death!

We mustn't tell Sister Sarah, Winnie!

Witchsongs

ON THE VOCATION OF SCHEMING WITCHSONGS, FOR THE MALLEABLE AND FOR THE UNYIELDING,

Through the siren songs of the witch, crops crisp on stalks and star-crossed furies fall in love. . . .

We sing in perfect harmony. We are the Daughters of Discord!

Very good, Sister Sarah. Though I prefer Daughters of Darkness.

Winnie, I love when you sing for your booook!

The Heart's Chord

ON THE WITCHSONG TO FALL IN LOVE,

A sibilant spell which beguileth distant souls to be enamored and forfeit for sake of love.

When cooed to the tune of a ballad,
One will exist with affection valid,
And begin a banter, with ogling eye
With full heart in thy hand, thy limit the sky.

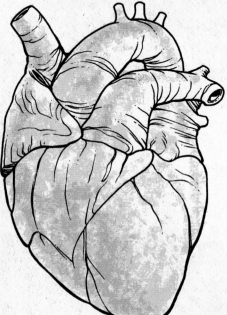

BEAT, LONELY HEART,
I'LL MAKE THEE SKIP,
AND SOFTEN THY
SPOT FOR ANOTHER
BEAT, LONELY HEART,
THE SPARK'S IN MY GRIP,
A LIFETIME TO SWEETLY
SMOTHER

Sisters! I am not getting any younger. The Life Potion!
Perhaps we can take the child from the Putnams . . .
or better yet, the Binxes.

The Mind's Chord

ON THE WITCHSONG TO CHANGE ONE'S MIND,

A cunning spell which captivateth clever minds
to assume thine advice and thy direction.

When sung to the tune of a jaunty air,
Thy victim obeyeth without a care,
To do as thou wilt, thine influence won,
The tide in thy favor when long day is done.

HARK, SACRED HOPES, I'LL GIVE THEE PEACE,
FOLLOW MINE ORDERS WITHOUT DELAY,
HARK, SACRED HOPES, THE WOOL'S IN THE FLEECE,
LET THINE INNER THOUGHTS FADE AWAY.

The Master's Chord

ON THE WITCHSONG TO SUMMON CHILDREN,

A cogent spell which beckoneth young ones
to pursue thy voice and thy fancy.

When sung to the lay of a lullaby,
All young souls who hear thine enchanting cry,
Are lost in a deep trance, till baleful deed is done,
Their essence yours to gasp when nowhere left to run.

COME, SLEEPY YOUNGSTERS, I'LL LEAD THEE AFAR,
INTO A REALM OF BEWITCHMENT,
COME, SLEEPY YOUNGSTERS, TRAIL MY BRIGHTEST STAR
FOLLOW MINE HONEYSUCKLE SCENT.

'Tis a song that couldst lure the children! They shall follow the candy-sweet scent of my song! I shall summon one of the Binx children at once! I shall start with the eldest boy. Thackery!

'Tis a wonderful scent of hyacinth and plumeria . . .
before all senses go bye-bye.

'Tis almost All Hallows' Eve. . . . The time draws near.
Go, Sister Sarah. Fetch a wretched brat from town. Not the Binx boy. The Binx girl! She is younger, with more life-force to sup. Go! Make haste. I shall ready the Life Potion. We shall be young and beautiful again.

Vow of the Red Witch

OW THAT THOU HAST STUDIED THY WORDS 'TIS TIME TO CEMENT THY TEACHINGS.

Once thou practicest all things laid out here within, thy spell book shall wipe clean, and replenish with pages anew, to convey thee on thy path of knowledge and witchcraft.

Come—thy crooked path hath but begun. Use these final pages to state thine intentions beyond this book and bind thyself to thy magick forevermore.

Perdurable Vow of Evil

Once you have read all thy book hath to give, recite this vow to confirm thine intent to carry out the teachings of these pages till thou meetest thy final fate.

The Vow
IN ITINERE INVENTIONIS
PENITAE PERREXI

We are young again!
But the townspeople have come for us!
Shall I prepare a swan song, sisters?

Ha! That will be the day, sisters.
We are witches. We are evil.
We are beautiful once again! We shall prevail!

Thou art so right, Winnie.
'Tis nothing carved in stone. Uh-oh. Bye-bye.

Here Scrawl Thine Own Vow. . . .

I vow to steal hearts and souls. —Gunnilda Arden

I vow to never apologize. —Odelina Arden

I vow to punish mine enemies. —Isolde Fitzrou

I vow to belittle mine adversaries. —Mathilda Picardy

I vow to lie and cheat. —Eve Harvey

I vow to deceive. —Amice Harvey

I vow to hold all grudges. —Frances Harvey

I vow to put beauty above all else. —Cecily Sanderisson

I vow to step on the necks of my competitors. —Emma Sanderisone

I vow to never have children. —Druscilla Sanderson

31st of October 1693
I vow to recapture my youth. —Winifred Sanderson

I vow to serve my dear sister Winnie! —Mary Sanderson

I vow to have boys fall in love with me! —Sarah Sanderson

LET the PAGES OF this BOOK REFLECT THY DEEPEST DESIRES. . . .